AN AFFAIR ABROAD

T.K. RICHARDS

You were the unexpected twist in my story, the plotline I never saw coming.

— UNKNOWN

EXCLUSIVE

This is the beginning of Nadia & Maximus's story. To learn more about these characters and receive bonus content, including a **bonus chapter, Second Honeymoon**, exclusive to my email subscribers. Sign up for my newsletter here:

https://tkrichardsnewsletter.ck.page
www.tkrichards.com

To the single ladies.
May you find love.

PROLOGUE

'*This is humbling. Sitting in a room full of strangers because I can't get over a man. What a bunch of losers. Wait a minute, I'm here so I guess I'm a loser, too. Why would I take advice from Carmen 'Can't Keep a Man' Woods? I would die if any of my friends saw me in here. Note to self— Give Carmen a tongue-lashing tomorrow— better yet, never mention I was here.*

I can barely hear myself think with Lady Chatterley sitting next to me. For the love of God, someone please shut this woman's mouth. I have been smiling and nodding the entire time she has been yapping her purple lips, but I haven't heard a word she's said.

Well what do we have here? This one seems pretty full of herself. I can tell from looking at her designer shoes whatever problem she's facing, it is most likely her fault. I shouldn't say such things. I don't know this woman, yet still I want to call her Ms. Look at Me. She can't stop looking in the mirror long enough to see what is actually happening in the world—like how I am intensely watching and judging her. Shame on me. A giant panther could have entered the room and she wouldn't know it. Look up sweetie you're not cute enough to be clueless.

My God! Who let King Kong out of her cage? Note to self, 'don't let her kick me in the ass.' She has to be the tallest, most statuesque white woman I have ever seen. Please don't sit by me, please don't sit by me. Whew! That was a close one. I might slip and say something slick and she would wipe the floor with me. Next mental note— Nadia, stop talking about these people.

Now what do we have here? Possible lesbians, perhaps? Jeez, I hope not. I can't bear to hear what issues they are having. I thought once you gave up on men, you should be happy by process of elimination. Right? How could any woman on woman relationship have problems when a man isn't involved? Guess I'll find out soon enough. If they do turn out to be a couple, I'll treat myself with donuts tonight. I beg someone, anyone, gas me now.

Is the therapist here already? Is she one of these women I have talked about horribly, waiting for the right time to speak? I don't want to be the guinea pig, nor do I want to sit here and waste my time looking at strangers all night. I have talked about them to myself which I really need to work on. Note to self— Work on your bullshit, and stop talking about people.'

NADIA

The metal door creaks as it flies open from the hands of a petite, well-dressed woman, rushing in with folders pressed against her chest. Her maroon-colored lipstick, and black cat-eye frames announced she was fashionable, and perhaps well paid, which was a good sign.

As her heels clanked across the wooden floor, I had a change of heart. This didn't seem like a place I belonged.

While the woman who had to be the therapist continued to get settled in, I stood up and grabbed my sweater from the back of my seat. I fixed my mouth to say, 'Sorry. I can't stay,' but before I could speak, the sharp dressed woman addressed the room.

"Forgive me for running late. I couldn't get my husband off of me."

She said it unapologetically, and smiled at everyone in the room.

'Wait, what? Did the therapist greet us with personal information? About herself? Maybe I will stay after all.'

I repositioned my sweater around my shoulders and made

myself comfortable, eager to hear what she was going to say next.

"Allow me to begin this session by asking you all a question. Are you open to sharing your deepest, darkest, most liberating sexual encounters with the people in this room?"

The room fell silent. We all looked around at each other with skepticism. Crickets chirping outside the windows, music from cars passing by, and chatter from the hallways filled the room as our whispers remained on pause.

"I urge you to answer my question honestly, as it is important for you to be successful with my methods. My name is Dr. Bartley, and I'm here to help you…help yourself."

She looked around the room, assessing us from what I gathered by her wrinkled brows and scrutinizing glare. No one found their voice to answer her question. Not a soul raised their hand to acknowledge the terms.

As the silence continued, Dr. Bartley wrote in her notebook, looking up at us above the rim of her glasses.

"I'm going to assume by remaining in your seat, that your response is yes. Yes?" Her eyes shift around the room. "Okay then. Let's get started." She pointed to the girl I nicknamed Ms. Look at Me. "You with the mirror."

"Me?" she asked, tapping her designer shoes.

Her heavy lined eyes looked confused. Her caramel face rosed a light hint of pink. Then, suddenly a bit of fear flashed in her eyes.

"Yes, you. You are primping in the middle of the day. Why?" Dr. Bartley questioned.

The girl scowled. "Don't you want to know my name first?"

"We'll get to names a little later. Right now, I'm interested in knowing why you are staring at yourself in the middle of the day? In a class for people who are sexually frustrated no less."

"Um, because you never know who you're going to meet," replied mirror girl.

"Did you plan on meeting someone to impress in here?" Dr. Bartley asked.

"Maybe."

"And how about you?" Dr. Bartley pointed her pen towards me.

I looked into her judgmental eyes. "What about me?"

"I saw you getting ready to leave when I walked in. Tell me why?"

"I had second thoughts about staying."

She grins. "Care to share why?"

Our eyes lock again as she attempts to bully me into submission.

"I don't think I belong in here."

"Then why did you sit back down?"

I smirk. "Honestly, when you blurted out that you couldn't get your husband off of you, I was intrigued. That was one hell of a way to enter a room."

My response creates a stir.

"I'm hearing you stayed because you're interested in other people's lives. Am I right?"

"I...I...I wouldn't use those exact words. I just found what you said to be very honest. You know. I have never met a person bold enough, or unafraid to enter a room as their true self. Nowadays, everyone is either faking it, or trying to be something they're not."

The room surprises me with support.

The girl I labeled as Lady Chatterley sat opposite of me, humming in agreement, catching the attention of Dr. Bartley.

"You appear to have something to add." The good doctor looked down her nose. "What brings you here?"

She stammered. "A former attendee recommended I sit in one of your sessions."

"Do you often take advice from unlicensed professionals?"

Lady Chatterley scoffed. "I beg your pardon."

"I'm asking you where is your own mind? Your own train of thought? Where is your courage to do what you think you should be doing? Don't worry. We'll work on those questions in the weeks to come."

Three of the seven attendees sat still with enthusiasm written on their faces. I assumed it was because Dr. Bartley hadn't put them on the spot yet. The two women I labeled a couple conversed with their eyes. Then, Lady Chatterley raised her hand to speak like we were in school.

"Can you start with someone else? Please? I don't want to go first."

Dr. Bartley replied with an impish grin across her lips. "Sure. Class, let me inform you. I am all about expressing how one truly feels. I encourage my class to speak freely and honestly. I will push you to stop hiding and reveal the person you are when no one else is around. Your true self. You will have to get personal, and dirty, and detailed in here. So, I ask you, is everyone in here comfortable with my methods? And this time I would like a verbal yes or no."

"Yes." Everyone answered except me.

"I was right earlier. I don't belong here. Good luck to you all," I said, avoiding direct eye contact with the room.

Quickly, I tossed my tote and sweater over my arm, and jetted to the exit so fast that I only heard my footsteps leading the way.

✈

FOR A WHILE I'd been second guessing myself about everything. I was taught to follow my gut, yet I ignored my instinct and sat back down.

'Big mistake. That's what my nosey ass gets.'

Nevertheless, I showed my face in there and gave it the old

college try. That was good enough for me, but not so much for my issue. Trust.

I went there to see if the good doctor could help me learn how to trust men again. How to move on from the man I fell head over heels in love with, that turned around and hurt me like I meant nothing to him.

Dylan Brentwood had me going in circles by the time we broke up for good. And all the head games he played with me, left me with more than a broken heart. I was left with mega trust issues, and it's been affecting my dating life.

So, trusting a room full of strangers with my most personal, intimate details and insecurities was not about to happen. I have my girls for that, but sometimes you can sense when they've had enough of listening to you go on about your no good ex-boyfriend.

'Too bad Dr. Bartley's session was a flop. I won't tell the girls I went there at the shower tomorrow. They already call me Naïve Nadia. No sense in givin' them more ammunition to use against me.'

THE PLAN

Despite the overcast and heavy weekend traffic, I wiggled my way through the backroads of Charlotte to Taylor's shower. Five minutes late, but on time before the bride threw a hissy fit, I arrived with the cheese and fruit tray, bottles of chardonnay, and tequila.

The bride and groom's side of the family filled the country club. Tables overflowed with gifts and cards. Libations spread across the room. And all of the attention was on Taylor, just the way she liked it.

Toward the end of the party, Levi King, the groom, swung by to collect the presents. While he cleared the venue, his bride-to-be, a few cousins, and our circle kept the party going. Some would consider us a lively bunch. They wouldn't be wrong.

Levi, the good guy that he is, didn't dare tear Taylor away from the spotlight. He packed up, waved his scrawny arms at us, and got the hell out of dodge.

The few of us that stayed behind snacked on the leftover food trays, and downed bottle after bottle. The amount of alcohol we consumed put Shannon, the outspoken, wild one, in rare form. She was always forward and unapologetically direct. But tequila was sure to amplify her loose tongue.

"Are you ever gonna tell us what he's like in bed?" She overstepped, but most of us chuckled anyway.

Isla's caramel hands snatched the near empty bottle of tequila from in front of her. "You are cut off for the night."

Taylor's amber face was flushed. She forced a smirk on her lips and stared into Shannon's glazed eyes. "You never share such information about the one."

Shannon's lighter shade of ginger face stiffened. Her golden eyes locked back on Taylor. Her lips curved into a sly grin. "He's that good, huh."

All of us squealed in high pitches that followed with roaring laughter. Taylor smiled so hard, her rosy cheeks gave us a break from her normal resting bitch face.

I could tell she didn't want to elaborate on her future husband, so I attempted to change the direction of the conversation.

"Taylor's right," I said. "It's none of our business."

"Then tell us what's going on with you and Evan?" Shannon asked, reaching over Isla for the bottle of tequila.

"Not a damn thing. I know you guys think he's a keeper, and yes he looks great on paper." I sigh. "But I am just not into him."

Taylor frowned at me. "Why not?"

Isla chimed in. "I wish a man like Evan would sweep me off of my feet."

"Look, I already feel bad about stringing him along. Trust me on this one. If you knew why I had to break up with him, you might sympathize with me."

Isla scowled in my direction.

Expecting them to take me at my word may have worked if they were of a sober mind. But on a drunken night, I could forget it.

"Then tell us why!" they demanded in unison like a rehearsed choir.

I finished off the drop of tequila in my glass, then chased it with a squeeze of lime between my teeth. Gasping from the burn, I strummed my fingers down the center of my chest, buying myself some time before I came clean.

"He is incapable of giving me an orgasm." I hid my face with shame, peeping at my friends through the cracks of my fingers.

Taylor and Isla shared a smirk. Khai raised her brows as she sipped from her glass. And Shannon couldn't help but be Shannon.

"Come again? No pun intended." Shannon chuckled.

I knew her too well to know her pun was indeed intended, and it received the laugh it deserved. Once the joke began to fade, I came clean.

"I've never had an orgasm with him. The sex is so horrible, I can't describe it. I can't fake it any longer."

Silence fell between us which is strange, because in this group, someone always has something to say—especially on the topic of men and sex. I studied each of their calculating faces, waiting to see who would speak first. I bet my money on Shannon and won.

"You're gonna let a good man go, because of bad sex. You're crazy, Nadia. Do you know the percentage of women who have to fake it in bed, but have a good man to come home to? Do you think a lot of women are sexually satisfied? Let me break it down for you." She slurred in a drunken stupor. "Studies show only twenty percent of people, married or single, actually experience the best sex of their lives. Get you a vibrator, handle your business, and keep that man."

"You seem to have it all figured out. Don't you, Sha?" I turned to Khai. "Pass the wine, please?"

Shannon continued her sermon. "You know I'm the one in this circle who knows the most about sex."

"Just because you talk about it the most, doesn't mean you know the most," Isla added.

"And you do?" Shannon pointed at Isla and scoffed. "As I was saying, Nadia, you better not throw a perfectly good man away when the rest of us are meeting pathological liars, cheaters, sword fighters, video game freaks, and whatnot." She stood and took a bow. "I rest my case. P.S. my advice is free of charge *this time*."

I balled up a paper napkin and threw it at her.

Khai, the level-headed one, finally decided to add her two cents. "Have you told him he was bad in bed?"

"No. I didn't want to hurt his feelings."

A collective sigh filled the room.

"If you were bad in bed he would definitely find a way to let you know," said Shannon.

"Right. Like stop calling or ghosting you," said Isla.

Shannon joked. "Girl, you said that like you got a lot of experience in that department."

While the two of them bickered, my thoughts trailed off at the truth of Shannon's words. Men don't consider a woman's feelings when making decisions. They're selfish. While women, on the other hand, curate their life based on a man. Girls choose a college based on a boy. Change their plans based on a boy. Accept public marriage proposals from men they don't like to spare him of embarrassment. The nurturer in us always spares a man's feelings. I know this firsthand.

I wasted my early twenties running behind Dylan. The asshole who I thought was the love of my life. I could have moved to New York City and become a dancer, or experienced the multicultural streets of The Big Apple and pursued my backup dream of being a writer at a major publication.

Instead, I met a big shouldered sexual God with a head full of coarse hair, and a smile that could charm the panties off a nun. It is because of him, I stayed in North Carolina after college—afraid if I left he would find someone better, or not want me anymore.

I was delusional to think distance would be the only reason he would cheat on me. And because of him, I have yet to trust a man with my heart.

I overanalyze everything in my relationships. His ghost lives rent free in my head, and his compulsive lying created a list of trigger words that make me question men's motives.

Evan is unlike Dylan in every way. I could trust him. He's kind, considerate, and successful. Like I said, good on paper. But I am bored out of my mind. Especially between the sheets. He's too good of a person to say that to. I'd rather his next girlfriend deliver that blow.

Khai put an end to Shannon and Isla going at it. She shut them up like she does her children and commanded the room.

"Nadia, I have to agree with Shannon. Evan is a catch *and* is crazy about you. I say fake it and stroke his ego, then get yours with a toy when you need it."

'Easy for a satisfied wife to say.'

The mention of a bedroom toy served as a segue for Shannon to boast about her solo missions, and recommend her favorite.

"All you need is a rose," she explains. "That thing have me traveling to space."

"Shannon please," Taylor interrupts, "Nadia, do you love Evan? Like at least a little bit?"

"I have love for him. But no. I can't say I love him."

Suddenly, Taylor's concerning demeanor changed. It transformed into her resting bitch face. Her brows crumpled and her eyes narrowed in on me.

"Y'all, she's trippin' on Dylan again. Look at her. She's still hung up on that douchebag after all this time."

"My breaking up with Evan is not about that asshole."

"Yes, it is." Taylor continued to embarrass me. "What is this hold he has on you? It's been five years, Nadia."

I was pissed Taylor brought Dylan into the conversation. She knew from the daggers my eyes threw at her, that I was not going to let it slide. When it was clear that I began to withdraw from the table, she tried to play nice, interrupting the million pieces of advice being handed to me.

"I'm in the minority, but I think Nadia breaking up with Evan was the right thing to do," she interjects. "If a guy isn't satisfying you in the bedroom, you will not take him seriously. I know I wouldn't." Her hands wave in front of me. "Look at you. Stunning and miserable. That combination doesn't pair. If Evan doesn't make you happy, he isn't the one. You want magic. And fire. And passion. I get it."

"Well, you just answered my question about your sex life." Shannon clinked her shot glass with the bottle she took back from Isla. "I'm happy for you, girl. May we all find that magic and fire you're talkin' about."

I raised my glass. "Cheers to that."

As I sipped from my flute, I thought about Evan and compared him to Dylan. With Dylan, my phone was glued to my hand. I made sure I didn't miss his call. I yearned for his touch in the middle of the day. Snuck home during lunch for quickies. I did none of that with Evan. I never looked for his call, and didn't care if our plans were cancelled.

Shannon giggled. "Dylan really dicmatized you. Part of me wants to say may that love never find me, but on the other hand, it makes me wonder what have I been missing 'cause I ain't never been crazy 'bout a man the way you are...I mean were about him. Shit! You've laid under a new one and still ain't got over your old one."

"She needs to lie under a better one," said Taylor. "Let us set you up with someone."

Shannon shook her head. "I'm not donating my reserve dick."

I sighed. "I don't want any of your hand me downs. I can find a man on my own, thank you very much."

Khai tapped my leg. "It's not about finding a man. It's about getting you laid with some good *D* so you can move on with your life. I know a guy so hung he gave me a bladder infection. You might be able to handle him. I sure couldn't."

"Thanks, but no thanks. I'll pass on the Emergency Room dick."

They laughed at me so hard, Isla spit out her drink. She had to stand to catch her breath. Taylor patted her back, then told everyone to lift their glasses.

"Let's make a toast. To Nadia finding a thoroughbred to blow out her back!"

Glasses clinked all across the table while I held my head low in humiliation.

"Now, before we say goodnight, we must discuss my seven-day wedding getaway." She squealed. "Here is the itinerary." Her cousin Janine passed out mini spiraled books with the London flag on the cover. "One week! Are y'all excited?"

Khai, long overdue for a break from motherhood, lit up. "I know I am."

"We are going to live like The Royals, or at least close to it," Taylor claimed. "Levi has rented buses, and a private chauffeur during our stay, along with scoring us access to clubs, and passes for a major festival happening while we're there."

Shannon danced in her seat. "That's what I'm talkin' 'bout. I'm ready to party like a rock star."

Taylor finished. "I beg you guys to please participate in the scheduled family games and activities. I promise I have everything spaced out so we can have a good time as well as rest and relax."

Isla scowled. "This says we're going to Paris."

"Yes. It's a two-hour train ride, so why not go while we're there."

I had been eyeing flights to Ibiza, Spain from London the moment Taylor announced her wedding plans.

I asked, "Will we have time to do something of our own choosing? I want to see the big magnetic rock, Es Vedra, in Spain. It's supposed to have healing powers."

"May it heal your broken heart," said Khai, squeezing my hand.

A line formed between Taylor's brows. "No. This is my wedding. We're doing everything I have planned. Look at the itinerary. We have a jam-packed week. You'll have to see Spain some other time."

I lost my buzz at how she dismissed me.

"Any word on what kind of men they have over there? Any extra Idris Elba's roaming around?" Shannon joked.

Isla slurred, "I heard a rumor that the men in London are the world's worst lovers."

"Welp, you all can expect a full-detailed report when we get back." Shannon chortled.

LONDON

*N*ever underestimate a bridezilla. When she says you won't have time for anything outside of the schedule she's curated, she means it.

Khai had my seat upgraded to first class. The long flight went smoothly. I landed in a new country and continent for the first time in my travels, eager to see the sites and take it all in. But as each member of the bridal party poured in, they were put to work.

'Not how I saw my arrival at all.'

By early evening, Taylor had all of the bridal party assembled in her suite. She wasted no time to give us our list of duties for the week, sucking the excitement out of the air. She ran a tight ship.

My order on the first night was to play hostess and welcome the guests at the reception in the hotel lounge. Not a bad job since I was able to scope everyone in house—get the first look at possible prospects.

Levi's family provided certifiable eye candy, and the week ahead felt promising for finding love where love was being celebrated, or at least a short-lived romance. If I had my say, there was one King boy that caught my eye, but if anything were to happen, he would have to approach me.

In between exchanging pleasantries with both families, Isla took it upon herself to ask the concierge about the Friday nightlife. According to the itinerary, we were scheduled to go clubbing Sunday night, but the girls and I were too excited to spend our first night in Europe stuck at the hotel.

We met in secret. Isla whipped out a list of events to check out nearby. When everyone was on board for a night out on the town, we agreed it was best to tell Taylor as a collective.

"The schedule says we're going clubbing on Sunday," she said.

Isla asked, "Why can't we go tonight and Sunday?"

"Levi and I have plans."

"Okay. And?" Shannon asked.

Taylor was thirty-eight hot to be excluded, but we didn't care. I already had my outfit picked out in my head while she stewed about us not following her itinerary.

To feel she was still in control, she gifted us the limousine for the night. We knew it was because she wanted to make sure we would be back in time to cater to her in the morning. Also, to boss us around.

The Fab Five became the Fab Four that night, and after a quick wardrobe change into skimpy outfits, we were at our first stop of the night a few blocks away from the hotel.

The pub on the corner was not what we had in mind. We sat in the back looking confused at one another.

Shannon screwed up her face. "Surely, the concierge didn't think *we* would have a good time here."

Isla scowled. "It looks empty."

"This scene is trite," I said.

"Trite?" The girls laughed at me.

I laughed too. "It seemed like the appropriate word to use being in London. I just hope the night isn't a total bust."

Isla asked Tony, our driver. "Are you familiar with any of the places on this list?"

He scoffed as he read. "With all due respect…You lot seem cheeky. This list is for tourists. A group of young ladies like yourself would enjoy the clubs the local heads go to."

We held a private sidebar conversation about what the hell cheeky meant, and what we should do. Tony still heard us.

Khai suggested, "I say we stick to the list. I'm not trying to be a human trafficking victim."

Isla snickered. "Who would buy and sell you Khai?"

Khai nudged her then added, "We're not home. We can't trust anyone. Not even Tony here, no offense." She motioned her head toward him.

He nodded.

Shannon mentioned, "Taylor said he is bonded and will be with us all week. I'm guessing we *can* trust him."

Khai questioned Tony, asking him a round of serious questions, instructed him to type out his full name and license number in an email to her sister, then made him swear he would do as we asked.

"I will take good care of your party. Would it be of interest to you if I drove by the scenes not mentioned on the list?"

The four of us nodded.

Khai added, "And Tony, Sir. I am live streaming this outing, so our whereabouts will be public."

"Sounds good, Madame." Tony placed a call on speakerphone. "Prano, mate. *Wagwan?*"

A high-pitched voice spoke lingo we didn't understand, while Tony explained our dilemma to him. At times, Tony sounded like the Prano character on the line. Both spoke with British accents but with different elocutions—alike yet different somehow.

Shannon leaned in. "Wherever that guy is sounds like the place we need to be."

Isla tapped Tony's shoulder. "Are we good?"

Tony tipped his hat. "I've got you in."

We arrived at Tower Nightclub. The place was in the middle of a busy block. The line to get in was down the street.

A bouncer controlled the scene, selecting those who could cross a velvet rope. Tony parked the limo directly in front of the entrance, and opened the door for us. The bystanders whispered as we crossed the rope, and like Shannon said, we were partying like rock stars—thanks to Tony's contact.

Once we were inside, Khai reminded us. "No woman left behind."

We shook hands, remembering the rules: No one goes to the ladies room alone, no one drinks from a glass you didn't see poured, and no one leaves without telling the group.

People of all shades were having a good time in the halls, on the floor, and at the bars. Techno rave tunes blasted through the speakers. The music scene was different from back home. Hot songs were blended with fast house tracks, heavy bass lines, and noisy effects. The club made it clear we were in the U.K.

Tony saw that we were settled at a table, then left us inside. A round of appetizers and cocktails were sent our way with a message, *'Welcome to The Smoke'.*

The music suddenly mixed with classic reggae dancehall, my favorite genre. Off I scurried to the middle of the dance floor.

I showed off my moves. Created my own space in the center. A crowd surrounded me as I threw my cilantro-colored fringe dress around so the tassels swung like weeds on a beach. I tossed my hair around as I was deep in the moment. I felt alive out there. It had been a while since I danced like I was being paid, and the cheering crowd and spotlight that appeared above me sent a pulse through me I couldn't fight.

I performed out there the way I would have if I had gone to New York. The surrounding crowd fueled my ego to carry on like it was the audition of a lifetime. Then, another dancer appeared within the darkness, either wanting to share or steal my light.

He circled me before he engaged. The beat dropped a dirty baseline, then he thrusted forward, winding on me from the rear. He placed his bulge against my ass. I turned around and frowned at him, getting a better look at who had the nerve to interrupt my set.

He wasn't anything to brag about. Nor was he close to being my type, but I couldn't deny he had rhythm in his blues.

I paused, giving him the spotlight to show what he could do. With my hands resting on my hips, I smiled at his acrobatic steps I couldn't compete with. So, he taunted me into a battle, thinking he could put me in my place.

I accepted his challenge, switching my moves to easy 1-2 steps and cute shoulder shimmies. But then, the music shifted to fast-paced hip hop, and I let loose. I circled the dancer, throwing my flimsy strands everywhere like I was a video vixen in the 90s.

Mr. Bojangles smiled at me as if we were old friends, then reached for my hand. We danced together like familiar compadres, creating a frenzy in the crowd. Back and forth we went as the end of the song neared. When I heard the transition of the next song being cued into the mix, I took my shining moment back and spun away from the dancer. My left leg rose slowly as I stood still. Then I held it up high and in place above my head for ten seconds while pretending to file my nails.

I surprised myself. Shocked that my twenty-seven year old body could still do the move I learned from watching Traci Young-Byron videos down in Florida.

After holding my balance and wowing the crowd, I lowered my leg and tossed my hair like an HBCU dancer in front of my opponent. He bowed down to me. I in turn curtsied, then he took my hand and squeezed it.

"You did that," he said, then kissed the back of hand.

"Why thank you. You were owning me out there. I had to do something."

We laughed like we were old acquaintances. The applause wound down and together we bowed, then walked off in opposite directions after sharing a brief hug.

I strutted back to my table for some much-needed rest, but before I could sit, Isla stood in front of me.

"Come with me to the ladies' room," she asked.

We snaked our way through the crowded halls. I looked behind us continuously, feeling as though we were being followed. A short, latte colored guy made eyes with me. I pretended I didn't notice him, and stood guard at the opening while Isla went inside the stall.

I debated if I should worry her about my suspicion as I fixed my hair in the mirror. I thought it could have been a coincidence that our eyes met in the crowd.

"You ready?" Isla asked me moments later.

I took a deep breath and nodded, leading the way back to our table. Just past the bar, a hand grabbed my arm. I jumped, recognizing the short man from the hall.

I moved his hand. "I saw you following us."

"Pardon me. I'm friends with Tony, the chauffeur who brought you here. Name's Hayden. But my friends call me Prano. I didn't mean to startle you."

His high-pitched tone of voice was easy to place.

"Nice to meet you, Prano. I'm Nadia, and this is Isla."

He nodded to us both. "Likewise."

I imagined him all wrong. A slim, tall, fair-skinned figure is how I thought he would look from his voice on the phone. But there stood a short cutie, grinning like a Cheshire Cat in our faces.

His eyes bounced between the two of us. "I hope you're enjoying yourselves. I planned on introducing myself to you ladies sooner, but business got in the way."

"Thanks for letting us in tonight," said Isla.

"My pleasure." He smiled on the side of his mouth revealing a dimple. "A few of my associates would like to meet you. I'll bring them to your table soon." He pointed at me. "But you have been asked to report to the deejay booth."

My face scrunched. "I beg your pardon?"

"The deejay asked me to find you. He wants to thank you personally for putting on a show out there. You have some really nice moves."

I blushed like an idiot. My cheeks were so full, they nearly burst. It was as if I had never received a compliment before.

"Thank you." My body twisted side to side. "If he really sent you out of your way, I guess we can go say hi." I looked to Isla for confirmation that it was okay with her.

"I guess it's okay." Isla shrugged her shoulders. "If he's fine, I call dibs."

That was her way of letting me know she wasn't getting stuck babysitting Prano all night.

"Isla, please," I said. "I'm not going there with you tonight. Besides, the man asked to meet *me*." I smiled at Prano. "After you."

"Right this way. I'll take you to the stage."

MAXIMUS

The side of the stage was guarded by a hefty security team, sectioned off by a wooden border with limited seating at the foot of the entrance. Prano climbed a few stairs to enter the booth. His back blocked my view of the deejay as he stood in the door.

It shut behind him when he climbed back down. He held up his index finger and mouthed. "He'll be out in a sec." A second turned to fifteen minutes, too long for Isla's liking.

She called Prano over. "Can you show us back to our table?"

His eyes grew wide. "I promise you. He'll be right out."

"You can show her back. I won't mind," I said.

Isla turned up her nose. "We don't roll like that. We travel in pairs. Always."

She was right. I was breaking the rule. But I wanted to meet the man who sent for me. I didn't care that song after song blasted in my ear from the nearby speakers.

"Five more minutes." I pleaded. "If he doesn't come out after two songs, we can go."

A line dance song came on next.

Prano tapped my shoulder. "When he plays this mix, he's

about to take a break. I promised him that I wouldn't let you leave. Just give him a few more minutes."

Isla interrupted, "Can you at least light a fire under him?"

Prano climbed the stairs back to the booth. He signaled a thumbs up when a second line dance song came on. He moved out of the way and an average height, slightly tanned white boy climbed down in front of him.

The closer he approached me, he wasn't so average height. He was at least six-foot-one, medium-build, with a head full of curly brown hair cut low on the sides and nape of his neck. He had thick eyebrows, hooded light-brown eyes, and a five o'clock shadow outlined his square jawline. A crisp white fitted t-shirt hugged his chest, and tailored white jeans hung correctly around his waist. The man looked like he stepped out of a Playgirl magazine. It was hard not to stare at him.

"Ladies, this is Mash. Mash this is Nadia, the dancer you asked to meet, and this is her pretty friend Isla." Prano smiled at her.

"Nice to meet you both, especially you." He kissed the back of my hand. "Dancing Queen."

I blushed, hiding my teeth from the gorgeous specimen. He glazed over me from head to toe, holding my hand like it was glued to his.

"Dancing Queen? Stop. I was just enjoying the music."

"Ah, an American. You surprise me yet again."

"I know we don't sound sophisticated like you Brits." I tilted my head. "You're easy to understand by the way. I was having trouble with your friend earlier."

He gazed into my eyes. "Ooh. I love your accent."

"I love yours."

I studied his full lips, then his eyes, then his lips, wondering what they taste like while I searched for the right words to say next. And how to say it being that my accent was all over the place at times. I had my home voice, which was country twang, my code switch work voice, and my Geechee tongue, which I spoke with my grandmother. Sometimes I spoke all three without realizing it.

"Tonight, must be my lucky night. A great beauty gave me the boost I needed to get through this set. You see, I just arrived back in the city for a big event this weekend. I'm fatigued to say the least. But you—You woke me up."

"Mash," I whisper. "I think I saw your name on the flyer for some big outdoor event we're going to tomorrow."

"Glastonbury?"

"Yeah. I'm here for a wedding. The bride and groom chartered a bus to get us there."

"That's where my next set is. As soon as I'm done here I'll load up and hit the road."

"Well I hope you get some rest some time in between."

He smiled at me, then glanced at his watch. "When is the wedding?"

I thought, *'Damn. Did I bore him?'*

Embarrassed, I set up my exit. "Next Sunday," I said, then began sliding my hand away from his. "Well, good luck tomorrow. It was nice meeting you." I looked into his eyes one more time.

He pulled my hand back. "Leaving so soon?"

"Yeah. We have to get some sleep. Long day tomorrow."

"Is this because I checked my watch?"

I pressed my lips together.

"My apologies." He smiled. "I was timing the song to see how much longer I can be right here with you."

Electricity shot through my body. "I don't wanna keep you from your work. And we really should be on our way since we have an early morning."

"You said you're here for a week?"

I nodded.

"If I give you my information, will I hear from you? I'd really like to talk with you some more. Maybe you could stop by my tent tomorrow. Check out my set?"

"I'd love to."

He handed me his card. "All of my socials are listed, and my mobile is on the back. I really hope I hear from you, Nadia."

I flipped over the card and grinned at the handwritten phone number on the back.

"You will." I lifted my head from studying the card.

His lips touched mine. He lingered. So did I.

'Was it accidental?' I wondered. *'He didn't pull away. Neither did I.'*

Our eyes locked and we shared a smile at our faux pas. Then, the song changed and he snapped out of the moment.

"I was aiming for your forehead, but you…I should apologize, but I don't want to," he said. "I'm not sorry."

"It's fine." I let go of his hand. "Don't miss your cue. I'll be in touch."

"I hope so," he said, then raced toward the steps.

"You ladies ready?" Prano asked.

"Yes," Isla answered for the both of us.

I followed her and Prano to the exit. Before we turned the corner, I looked back for another glance of my admirer. He stood at the top of the steps, watching me walk away. Our eyes met in the short distance, and he flashed me his million dollar smile before the stage door closed.

I turned the corner as he caught his queue, and something in my soul told me the song that he played next was for me.

SOUTHERNPLAYALISTIC

A sped up version of Bob Marley's *Is This Love* had the entire club singing. I'm not sure if I walked, skated, or floated back to our table. I felt like I was in heaven. My body tingled all over. This was the first time I found a Caucasian man attractive. And to share such chemistry with a total stranger had me out of sorts.

Men of different persuasions made passes at me before, but I never flirted back. I never gave them a chance, or a second look. But this Mash character had some sort of power over me.

I actually waited around to meet him—something I wouldn't have done back home. I couldn't believe I engaged with a smoldering, brown-eyed babe, the color of buttermilk. And he had my stomach in knots.

Prano greets the table. "Hello. Nice to meet you ladies." He turned to me. "I overheard you say you needed to leave. When you are, let me know and I'll have Tony pull your car around. I'll be right over there."

I slipped my cell number in his hand. "Give this to him for me. Please. Thanks for everything, Prano."

"Who is this? And where the hell did you two slip off to?" Shannon asked.

Isla filled the girls in on our whereabouts. I didn't challenge her version of events as my head was so far up in the clouds, I could lay on one.

Shannon snapped her fingers. "Nadia, I know you're tired after all of that gyrating out there. And now we're hearing you were backstage making out with strangers?"

"What? I didn't make out with anyone. It was an accidental kiss." I side-eye Isla. "And what's with the plural exaggeration? It was one guy."

Isla leaned forward. "A white guy."

I zoned out, replaying that kiss. The feel of his lips. The way his eyes shone when they looked into mine. The way I wanted to ditch my friends, force my way back into VIP, and taste him once more.

Shannon woke me from my trance with a light nudge. "You fly out of the country one time and now you're swirling?" She laughed. "Can't take you nowhere."

I looked past her, and stared at the dark deejay booth. I imagined he was looking at me as I was trying to look at him.

"We should get going," said Khai. "The last thing we want to do is be late tomorrow after going out tonight."

Isla snapped her fingers and summoned Prano. "We're ready for the car."

He nodded. "If you need anything, want to know the happening places, or looking for a good time, tell Tony to give me a call, and I'll spot you lovely ladies."

"We'll remember that, Prano," said Shannon.

I took one last look at the stage, and followed the girls back to the car.

THE GIRLS HOUNDED me on the way back to the hotel. I kept quiet. It was something about the night, the music, and that man that made me want to keep how I was feeling to myself. I was mystified at my intrigue of someone so fast.

Thankfully, Khai was too tired to badger me once we made it back to our room—or so I thought.

"Don't think your slick ass is off the hook." She giggled. "I want answers in the morning," she said, then dozed off.

A mixture of sleep and restlessness shared space in my body as I stretched across my bed, unable to pull myself out of my daydream. That kiss moved me.

My phone buzzed with an unrecognizable number on the screen. I knew Prano came through for me.

> I'd like to see you before I get on the road.

> Can I stop by?

I froze. I wanted to see him. I wanted to say yes, but feared I would appear desperate in his eyes. And then, there was the fact I would be alone with him. At a late hour no less.

I took too long to respond, so he sent a follow-up message.

> I hope I didn't wake you.

I held the phone to my chest while my mind shuffled words to reply.

> You didn't wake me.

I backspaced that out.

> I want to see you too.

'Too forward.' I deleted that response, too. *'What do I do?'*

I was in London, on a destination wedding vacation with love in the air. I just experienced the most fun I'd had in a long, long time, and a possible connection had my emotions all over the place. I looked at his last message, listened to my gut, and leapt.

I'm at The Mandarin in Hyde Park.

I took a fast, hot shower, washed off my make-up, brushed my teeth, and moisturized my face so he could see me in my natural state. I slid into the pair of jeans from the top of my suitcase and a fitted tee, then applied some lip balm so my lips wouldn't be dry in case we kissed again.

My phone chimed.

I'm in the lobby.

I pulled my hair up into a ponytail, slipped on my flats, grabbed the room key, then eased out of the room to not wake Khai.

My heart raced as I walked to the elevator. When the doors merged together, I felt conflicted about my decision. I thought, *'I should have made him wait to see me,'* but it was too late for that. I was already on the ground floor, and there was no turning back. My heart won this round, and my brain would have to take the loss.

There he stood near the front desk. His back was turned as he perused the lobby. I made my way over and plopped in front of him. He didn't say anything when he saw me. He smiled and dropped his head.

Nervously, I began twisting and turning about, and starting smiling back at him.

"My crew is out front giving me hell for coming over here."

The bass in his voice nearly made my knees buckle.

He grinned. "But I had to. I couldn't stop thinking about you. I had to see your face. Even if it's only for a few minutes."

"I'm flattered."

He ran his hand over his head. "You make me nervous. Do I make you feel the same?"

"A little."

"That must mean something. Right?" he asked with seduction in his eyes. "I hope we find out what that something is."

I was tempted. By him. By his accent. The way he talked drove me wild. That deep baritone spitting game like romance was his profession—and the five o'clock shadow filling on his face made it easier for him to reel me further into his abyss.

"That would be nice," I said.

He put his hands in his pocket. "I'm normally cool. Forgive me for staring. There's something about you...I can't...take my eyes off of you."

My face burned from his flattery. "Ya know, you didn't have to come all the way over here to see me. I could have sent you a picture."

"It wouldn't have been the same."

My head tilted. "Why not?"

"Because I can't kiss a picture," he said, then stole my lips.

He looked into my eyes, and placed his full lips against mine in a delicate manner. He pulled away, holding my gaze, then came back in for a second kiss. I met him halfway to return the gesture and closed my eyes. I had to because the longer I looked at him, the wilder my thoughts ran.

I reveled in the trace of liquor that mixed well with the sweetness of his tongue. His hand was wrapped around mine by the time our locked lips separated, and it was nothing short of perfection. Just like the night.

He moaned. "That was exactly how I imagined it."

"Sounds like you got what you came here for."

His associate entered the hotel and signaled it was time to

hit the road. Our hands unlocked, but his pinky finger intertwined with mine.

"Thanks for letting me. I know what I'll be dreaming about on the bus." He pecked me one last time. "I'll tell you about it when you come see me tomorrow." He slowly backed away and freed my hand.

"I look forward to it. Good night."

I walked backwards towards the elevator. He walked backwards to the exit. He waved goodbye, then called out to me across the empty lobby.

"Nadia! I've changed my mind! Send me a picture!" he said, as the steel doors closed between us.

PUBLIC DISPLAY

$\mathcal{T}$he bus to the festival was interesting, especially the seating arrangements. Taylor assigned seats like we were children on a field trip. The groom's family on the left. The bride's family on the right. The majority of us laughed her off and sat where we pleased.

For two and half hours, the ride was loud, then quiet, bumpy, then smooth. Some of us read. Some of us played cards. Some of us got crafty with the drink, and some of us slept.

I was of the latter, drifting off into dreamland below an itchy blanket from the closet in my room. The sweetest of dreams filled my head as I caught up on rest, then woke up to country terrain leading into Glastonbury.

I panned out my view in the window and caught a glimpse of myself in the reflection. A light smile was plastered on my face. It grew bigger once I recognized it, like my mouth was stuck in an upward curved pose.

"You good?" Khai asked.

"Yeah. Why?"

"No reason."

"I'm ready to get off this bus and stretch my legs."

"I'm surprised they're not sore from last night."

I leaned into her laughing. "I might not dance anymore, but I still work out."

The bus parked dropped us off as close as it could to the gate. My stomach ached with butterflies fluttering in circles. My chest tightened with knots. I didn't know what to say to Mash when I saw him after dreaming up fairytales all night.

The field was packed with free-spirited party goers. The scene reminded me of Coachella. We trekked at least a mile in the entrance line. I grew nervous the event would be over by the time we made it inside.

While it took forever to get through the long line, I tended to my emails and submission posts, then called Mash to let him know I'd arrived. My call went straight to voicemail.

Naturally, I assumed the worst. *'He's blowing me off. He's probably with a groupie. He's changed his mind,'* I thought.

I had plenty of time to cook up all things negative while the day slipped away to make into the park, and another twenty minute walk through a mega crowd to the main stage.

Taylor and Levi asked the group to huddle before we went our separate ways.

"Be careful. Have fun. Don't get into any trouble 'cause we're not bailing anyone out. And meet back at this gate at 10:00. Y'all got it?"

"Got it!"

"Now let's go party!"

Khai said to me, "I'm following you."

"As if I would complain about that."

"And you can tell me why you've been smiling all damn day."

I told her about the lobby kiss while we searched for Mash's tent. Along the way we had our horoscopes read, caught a contact high in a trip hop tent, and watched snippets of a few shows by bands we never heard of—making note of who to follow.

Khai and I have always been open-eared enthusiasts, and closer to one another within the group. She is the one I could tell my secrets to, and they'll never get back to me. She's also the one that can talk me off a ledge when I'm about to crash out.

"I hope your mystery man plays some good music like he did last night. I can't wait to meet him. Do you think he'll mind that you brought me with you?"

"I don't see why he would. It's not like we're on a date or anything. He'll be working anyway."

Marijuana began to swarm the gardens. Slightly stoned, or maybe heavily, we footed the fields and finally found the tent.

I said to Khai. "I'm nervous."

"I can tell. Now I really wanna meet him.

With sweaty palms, I texted him, hoping he wasn't ghosting me.

I'm outside.

The three dots formed on the bottom of my phone screen and I shrieked on the inside.

Come to the back of the tent by the loading truck.

We entered through flimsy drapes next to a fired up generator. Eyes from every direction shifted toward us. Two huge security guards blocked the view. One of them furrowed his brows and bared his teeth at us.

The other said, "Don't mind him. He's harmless. Are you ladies lost?"

"Nadia!" A voice shouted to our right.

Khai and I followed it.

"They're with us!" Prano yelled.

The guards let us pass, and my bestie and I joined a crowd

behind the stage full of notable talent, socialites, and a few famous faces. They sneered. Khai and I sneered back as Prano led us to an open VIP seating area, roped off by a metal chain and equipment.

As he repeated, "Excuse us. Excuse us," a bad childhood habit resurfaced. I began mocking his accent, horribly I might add.

Khai looked at me shivering with giggles. "Now is not the time. What are you doing?"

"I'm not doing it on purpose. Make me laugh or something so I don't do it in front of..."

Mash leaned down to kiss my cheek. "Hey, beautiful."

His hand wrapped around my waist. I nearly melted from his touch. The way he looked at me made my chest pound so fast and hard, I lost my breath. I feared I could lose control with him. Be wild and carefree without the morning after regret and remorse.

To break the spell being casted on me, I asked him, "What is your real name?"

"Maximus Sharper."

'Mmm, a strong name,' I said to myself.

"Let's get you off your feet."

He led me to a sofa behind a curtain. The area was visible to the VIP area, but an inch more private.

I joked. "So the VIP has a VIP."

He laughed. "You can say that."

My left leg crossed his right leg as we sat close on one corner of the couch. Khai and Prano followed us to the exclusive area. Khai sat in the middle. Prano took up space on the other side.

"Since we're giving out surnames, what is yours?" Mash asked.

"Melton."

"Melton? I don't think I know any Melton's." His hand traced circles on my thigh while the other reached for my hand. "Nadia Melton."

I stared into his eyes as he crooned out my name. "So, did you dream about me?"

"I dreamt about our kiss."

"So did I."

Khai glanced at me from the corner of her eyes. I watched them trail down to my leg, and grinned at the look on her face as Mash fondled my thigh. He brought me back into the moment by leaning in closer.

"Is it too soon for another one?" he asked.

"No, sir."

He pulled the hem of my t-shirt, inching me toward him. Lightly, his fingers swept around the back of my neck, then he planted his succulent lips against mine. I gulped in his air as he took in mine. We put on a public display of affection, and like a schoolgirl, I counted the seconds, never wanting it to end.

Heat sparked between us. Neither of us attempted to pull back. I shifted my body, placing my knees across his lap, while my hands held onto the mound of his shoulders.

Khai cleared her throat once or twice. I was too occupied to recall the exact number.

She raised her hand. "I'm Khai, by the way."

We turned toward my good friend. I wiped my lipstick from Mash's mouth and snickered.

"My bad, sis. Mash this is my best friend, Khai. Khai, this is Maximus, also known as Mash."

"It's nice to put a face with a name." She smiled. "I haven't seen my friend smile like this in a long time."

"I like the sound of that." He shook her hand. "Nice to meet you."

"All is forgiven." Her eyes gave me the approval look. "Prano and I are going to give you two some privacy. But not too much. Alright?"

Mash held up his hands. "I promise I'll behave."

Prano and Khai disappeared behind the curtain.

"But I don't want to," he whispered in my mouth.

We shared a laughable lip embrace, then cooled things down as his set was coming up. Twenty minutes of conversation, flowing energy, and explosive chemistry felt like magic surrounded us. Our words connected like a game of scrabble, and our souls touched by simply gazing into each other's eyes.

The show coordinator called for him. Our beautiful moment was put on pause. I already missed studying his mind behind his eyes. I could look into them for seven days and seven nights, and listen to his voice convince me to do whatever he wanted.

He helped me from the couch. "Have dinner with me tomorrow night?" He stole one last kiss.

The question brought visions of me pressed beneath him with erotic expressions and joy on my face. My hands on his chest, pushing him back as it's all too much.

His hand stroked my cheek. "Nadia?"

I snap back to reality. "Yeah."

"Was that a yes?"

"Yes. What time should I be ready?"

"Pick you up at seven."

He walked me to the side of the stage.

Khai hops up. "You ready?"

My head nodded, but my mouth said, "No."

We leave before Mash's name is announced, trekking our way back to the meeting point. Out of nowhere, the two of us are bum-rushed by a marijuana mob carrying us away in their flock. We held hands to stay together as the weirdness of the crowd grew by the minute.

I was mortified by painted faces screaming shit I couldn't make out. Khai and I had to fight our way out of the high horde and drunken pack.

"If ever there was a sign that it is time to go." Khai grabbed my arm.

"Say that again. I'm spent."

"You should be, after all that mixing up on that couch."

I beamed brighter than the moon lighting the field. And after a long flight, a night of dancing, a catnap, a drive to the countryside, walking miles at a festival, and getting fresh with a handsome man riling me up, that light within me didn't fade. It carried me through the next day of bridesmaid responsibilities, and gave me the energy to get dolled up for my date with Mr. Sharper.

LOVE TO SEE IT

I was behaving recklessly. I gave zero fucks about any opinions regarding going on that date.

It was unlike me to participate in public displays of affection. To go against our girlfriend's rule of traveling in packs. To kiss a man I've known less than an hour. It was a good thing Khai and I shared a room. If I had it to myself, I didn't trust that both of my feet wouldn't have been off of the floor before our date started.

Khai was concerned that the dress I chose to wear was overly, sexually enticing. She placed it back on the hangar and unzipped the bag with a blue, one-piece jumpsuit inside. The open neckline accentuated my healthy bosoms just enough according to her, and the loose lines in the pants fell in the right places to show my curves.

Since this was a special occasion, I accessorized with my custom Billie Hilliard bracelet cuffs, and chose three-inch strappy heels for style and comfort. I placed my flat shoes in my oversized purse, and when Khai wasn't looking, I threw in my toothbrush, a pair of panties, some leggings, and my make-up bag.

Maximus knocked on the door. My heart fluttered with anticipation like a teenage girl going on her first date. I became giddy knowing he was on the other side of the door—quietly stomping and silent screaming to get out all of the nerves.

"Can I open it now?" Khai asked.

I composed myself and nodded, making a mental note, *'Don't over talk, don't mimic his accent, be present, listen for any lies, and don't say anything stupid.'*

Khai opened the door.

"Damn," I muttered, verbally fumbling before I got one foot out of the door.

The man was fine as hell. His light brown eyes glistened in the low lights. He pulled one of the roses from a bouquet and handed it to Khai when he greeted her.

"I see my date is ready." He smiled at me as I grabbed my sweater. "These are for you."

"Thank you." I passed them to Khai and mouthed. "Don't wait up."

"Shall we?" He hooked his arm around mine. "Blue is your color."

"I'll keep that in mind."

He pressed the button for the elevator and kissed me while we waited. Within seconds, I was wrapped in his arms, inhaling the orange notes of his cologne. The scent blended well with his natural scent that had me thinking, *'take me now.'*

I clung to his manliness, admiring the sharp way he was dressed for the evening. For me. His garments looked tailored. Fitted black slacks and a black pullover, with a light blue and black oxford shirt peeking above the collar.

I held on to him so tight, I knew he could tell I didn't want to let go when the elevator opened. He had me in his clutch. The question of the night was if he knew it.

On the ride down, I pictured my fingers stroking his freshly trimmed beard while he lied on top of me—fucking me slow.

The bell dinged and I had to check my nipples for budding activity. It was clear I couldn't trust myself around Maximus, and I was grateful Khai was present to block me from spreading wide eagle like a happy harlot.

She liked Mash from what she knew of him in the short span. But she didn't trust that we were not on home soil, or that he could be pretending to be a nice guy who actually fronted a traffic ring. "You never know," she said, on the way back from the festival. "When you go out with him tomorrow, make sure you ping me every hour."

I agreed to do it. It was smart. And her way of saying she loved me. Khai being the wife of a cop, made me take all of her safety tips seriously. But something in my gut told me she was worried for no reason that night.

Mr. Maximus Sharper demonstrated grown man, BDE. He escorted me around his city in a vintage town car, and made eye contact with me when he spoke. Little things like placing his hand in the small of my back when we walked, holding my hand, and knowing how to hold a conversation added to his good looks. I was afraid he was too good to be true.

Before dinner, he explained the significance of well-known tourist attractions. I nodded as if I understood. It had something to do with the restaurant where we dined. All I could think about was how he pulled out my chair, stood until I was seated, and rose when I left the table to wash my hands.

"I'm curious about the fish and chips," I said.

"Don't they sell it where you're from?"

"They do. But I'm wondering if it tastes better over here."

He ordered it as an appetizer. "I'll let you be the judge." He smirked. "But also order something else from the menu. I planned to share my dish with you anyhow."

I was a fan of how he took charge, just as he did our first kiss.

Afraid I was going to humiliate myself, or say something

stupid again, I kept quiet at dinner. It created an awkward vibe. He took notice.

"Is something wrong?"

"No."

"You seem withdrawn."

I took a deep breath. "I'm not feeling like myself, honestly. I convinced myself to not talk too much so I won't ruin tonight."

He reached for my hand. "If I have any say, I'd prefer the real you. The woman that's made me happy the past few days." He laughed at my honesty. "I thought I had done something wrong."

"Far from it."

"So tell me more about you."

I talked his head off. He heard about my failed career attempts, my childhood dream of becoming a famous dancer, my backup interest of writing professionally, and how my last real relationship was five years ago.

He didn't judge me for stuffing my face in between each story. He listened. Not only with his ears, but also with his eyes.

"I have a confession," I said. "I have never been in the company of a man like yourself."

"What do you mean?"

I sipped my water. "Not Black."

He sat back with a line between his brows. The silence cut the cord of conversation that had been perfect all night. I told myself, *'Well at least you got a good meal, a private tour of the city, and a few good kisses on this trip.'*

"Shit," I whispered. "This is why I told myself to not talk too much."

"You're a bit hard on yourself, aren't you?"

"At times. And this is why. I've been too honest and now you're acting all distant."

Fumbling his fingers against the white tablecloth, he stared at me. I looked away, afraid he was about to end the night early.

"If I may put an ease to all of that you have going on over

there, I want you to know I wasn't offended by what you said. I'm actually flattered to be the first White man you've spent time with." He chuckled. "What took you so long?"

We laughed the tension away.

"Why'd you give me a chance?"

"Now here is where I really should be quiet."

"I beg to differ. Tell me."

"It feels strange saying this. Not to mention too early, but there is something about you that I feel drawn to. I wish I could articulate it better, but it's like there aren't any words to describe this feeling. But it exists. Ya know." I exhale. "I probably sound crazy right now."

"You don't." He smiled at me with his eyes. "I feel it too."

My spine tingled. To distract the way I wanted to jump across the table and express what I was unable to say, I swirled my glass of wine in front of my lips, sniffed it, then sipped.

"Are you comfortable being seen with me?" he asked.

"Are you with me?"

"Why wouldn't I be? You're fucking beautiful. And since we are talking about this, you may as well know, I have gone out with women of all persuasions, but you are the first to have this effect on me."

"And I've been approached by men like you, but I never accepted. Until now."

Fast and hard, I was falling. And I was terrified that my heart was going to get broken. In the back of my mind, I thought the only thing that could save me was the rumor about British men being horrible in bed. That riddle was one hundred percent getting solved that night.

He patted his belly. "Feel like going for a walk?"

"I'd love to."

Maximus got a good chuckle when I slipped on my flats. He led me down lesser crowded streets in the city, stroking my hand with his fingers during our stroll. We talked for blocks and blocks, ducking in and out of the main streets. The background noise of traffic grew heavier the closer we approached Buckingham Palace. Yards away from the courtyard, gold and white lights lit the site so bright, I could see it clearly from where we stood.

A night breeze wrapped around us. Mash placed his jacket around my sweater, protecting me from the night air turning on its chill. As I marveled at the historic palace, the glimmer in my eyes lured him in.

He kissed me in the moonlight. The intensity between our lips screamed he wanted more of me, and I needed more of him.

He pulled away. "Are you ready to go back to the hotel?"

"No. But if you need to get some rest I understand."

"Rest is the last thing on my mind." He gazed into my eyes.

"So, where to then?"

"I'd love to show you my place?"

"I'd love to see it."

INDIGO

Not quite an hour from the city, we drove miles and miles into the suburbs down curvy roads and dark streets to Maximus's house. After many hillsides later, he entered a code at a gate, then drove another two miles inside a private neighborhood. It was dimly lit with street lights few and in between, and at least three or more acres separated each home.

The houses were monstrous. I grew anxious to see where we would end up. Finally, he turned into this beautiful mini-castle. It'd be easy to miss with the exterior mild lights hiding it from the road.

His house sat on greenery for days. I thought to myself, '*He must be one hell of a deejay to afford something like this.*'

My small, three-bedroom starter home could fit inside his colossal house. Suddenly, I felt out of my league. Not worthy to be associated with someone of his means.

He opened my car. "Far enough out of the city for ya?"

"I'm not the one who had to drive." I lift up at the pull of his hand.

"Well, this is me."

I raise a brow. My first thought is, *It's a lot of...you.* I scratch that and think, *It's a lot of house for one person.* I didn't dare say that aloud. "It's beautiful," I said, with a smile.

"Thanks. I bought it on a whim. I was thinking of downsizing next year, but I really like this area. Shall we go inside?"

"Please." I pause my steps. "Do you have any dogs?"

"Not since Blue died two years ago."

I rematch his pace forward. "Sorry. I just like to be prepared. Sordid history in that department."

"No worries." He opened the door to his palace. "Come. Let me show you around."

The first room we entered was his man cave/studio that sat at the bottom of the house off of a narrow hallway from the three door garage. Collectible toys lined across shelves on one wall opposite a bar for hosting. Next to it was a pool table, then a Styrofoam recording room occupied the corner. Leather furniture, LED lights mounted all around the room, and framed awards of his accomplishments hang on the back wall.

"Nice," I said. "You're a big star and I had no clue."

"Another reason why I like you."

I tease him, walking out of the room. "Do you, now?"

A light laugh tickled his throat. "Shall I show you the bedrooms?"

I hesitated for a brief moment. "Of course."

He talked more during the tour of the city than he did his home. He announced bedrooms 1-4, let me walk around and ask questions, and he answered them. Heading into the workout area near the living room, abstract paintings, and floating shelves hung on the walls. The decorum was inspired by Indian culture.

"I admire your taste. Did you do the interior design?"

"I hired professionals."

"Well, they did an excellent job. It's clean. Modern. And sexy. But where are you in here?"

"I don't understand."

"Where are the pictures of you? Your family? Your moments?"

He avoided looking at me and murmured, "My moments. Hmm. Photographs belong in photo albums, not walls. Watch your step." He took my hand and led me into an open floor plan living room where a massive, curved screen television rose from the floor. "Ask me how many times I've turned that thing on?"

"How many?"

"Once. The day it was installed. I hardly have time to watch tele."

I gathered I should have been impressed, but I wasn't. All men are fascinated with oversized TVs, fast cars, and the latest electronic gadgets. To the right of the T.V., an electric fireplace had a protective screen as big as the one on the tube. I desperately wished he turned it on, but I kept quiet, not wanting to overstep my first time as his guest.

The house was undeniably beautiful, but nippy. I chanted to myself, *'Let's stay in here. Turn on that heater.'* Getting warm in front of the fire felt like the perfect place to lounge and continue our conversation.

I tugged on my sweater, hoping he'd notice. I assumed he did when he took one of the decorative fur throws from the sofa, and wrapped it around me. I assumed wrong. He covered me because we climbed five steps from the left side of the living room, and walked through double glass doors to an indoor pool area with a retractable roof.

I couldn't see the landscape, but I imagined it was beautiful the way the grass glistened and light bounced off the ground. We cuddled under the fur blanket, admiring the stars through the open roof. The moon's reflection hit the waves in the pool, giving his brown eyes a glow that held my attention.

We conversed about music, movies, our likes and dislikes, and cultural differences without any regard of the time.

"What is your favorite song of all time?" he asked.

"Ugh, that's a hard one. I love so many different genres."

"But there has to be one song you love more than any other piece of music. When I asked the question, what song popped into your head?"

I blurted, "Sting, *When We Dance*."

"Voila, your favorite song of all time."

"Is it though? I mean I do love it. It's definitely in my top five. What's your favorite song?"

"Bob Marley, *Waiting in Vain*."

"Ooh, that's a good one."

His face lit up as he grinned. "It is, isn't it?"

A breeze of cold air infiltrated the blanket. I shivered. His warmth drew me in closer, and I pressed my head against his chest for comfort.

He squeezed my shoulders. "I'm assuming you like reggae music...judging by your moves from the other night."

"Very much so."

"What's your favorite Bob song?"

"*Chances Are*."

He scoffed. "You keep surprising me."

"How so?"

"I thought you were going to name a commercial, more well-known track by The Great Late."

I'd run out of words, thinking what Bob song I could try to sing to blow his mind. I'd been quiet so long, he stared at me. Still unable to moan or hum a tune, I settled and looked into his eyes. I wondered what he was thinking when he took me by the face and kissed me so tender I felt a tingle in my chest.

"You're freezing." He rubbed the coldness of my cheeks. "Let's go inside."

He closed the rooftop, then escorted back into the living

room. He flipped a switch and a red and brown fire formed behind the black glass. I sat in front of it on a stone colored rug, nestled in arms below the blanket until it was no longer needed.

The tender kiss he planted on me outside escalated to full blown passion, sparking heat of our own. My sweater was tossed. His sweater disappeared. And the flames from both the fire and us turned the once cold room into a sweltering sauna.

Respectfully, he fought the urge to explore me as I unbuttoned half of his oxford shirt. I found his restraint admirable. Especially since he was third base hunching me on the carpet. So, I played his game and stopped undressing him.

"You didn't finish giving me the tour," I said.

He pulled me up from the rug, never letting go of my hand. "I've shown you everywhere except the kitchen and the master." He looked at me, then turned away when I caught him.

I would have paid a million dollars to read his mind. I guessed he was confused why I pulled the brakes in the living room, and wondering if he brought me all this way for me to end up being a tease. I wanted to give in to him, just not on his living room floor.

Outside of the dining room, he paused in the hallway. I was pressed against the wall and felt up like my body told him it was what I wanted. Mash stole soft kisses from me. The feel of his hands digging into my lower back withdrew a sigh I couldn't hold in.

His bulge tightened against my stomach. I tipped up on my toes to ease the pressure of it on the verge of busting loose.

I motioned my head to the room up ahead. "Is that the kitchen?"

He grunted.

I slid out from him and led him to the room. "Now this is a kitchen," I said, wiping my mouth.

"I've used the stove maybe twice, and I've never used the oven."

"Seriously? I could get fat in a kitchen like this. You have everything. I mean literally everything."

"Yeah, but it's no fun cooking for one." His eyes followed me.

"That is so true. I cook and invite my crew over to eat all the time."

"So, you cook a lot?"

"Cook and bake."

"I hope I get invited to one of those dinners. I'd like to see you in action."

"Trust, I can burn."

His head wavered. "You can what?"

"Burn. Where I'm from it means I cook really well. Slang, AAVE, or the less popular term, Ebonics, is what some would call it. I might whip up something for you while I'm here. Umm, do I spy another pool table?"

He looked behind him. "That's the dining room, but as you can see the table is all that's in there."

I bit my lip. "A pool table is sitting where a dining table should be. It screams bachelor pad." I chuckle, circling the table and making him chase me.

"What can I say? I love the game. It's my favorite pastime, and my stress reliever. Sometimes I don't want to walk all the way downstairs, so I put another table in this empty space."

"You don't owe me any explanations about your house. But the fact that you did, has earned you some bonus points. Besides, it is still a table, right?"

"Right. I knew you were smart." He closed in on me. "You're the first person to ever walk through my entire house."

"Come again? A house this beautiful? And I'm the only one?"

"It's true. I've been here a little over six months, and you are the first."

I couldn't look him in the eye. It was hard to believe he hadn't had a woman stay over and roam through his house—fuck in this house.

I avoided his gaze and used his words from dinner. "Why me?"

"Did you hear me say I liked you earlier? There's a vibe between us." He catches up to me. "Say you feel it, too."

My mouth said, "I feel it." My mind said, *'This man better not be playing with my emotions?'*

He kissed my neck. "When will I get to see your house?"

And there it was. His second time referencing he wants to visit me back home. I panicked at the suggestion and prayed in my head, *'God, I hope he is for real.'*

"My house? You'd be disappointed. It's cozy, and clean and decorated to my taste, but it's nothing compared to yours."

"Something you should know about me is I say what I mean, and I mean what I say. I felt a connection with you the moment I saw you. I couldn't take my eyes off of you. The only reason I let the song you were dancing to play all the way through is because I didn't want you to stop dancing. Or for it to be the last time I saw you. No one has ever had this effect on me. Ever."

I confess. "I haven't felt close to anyone for a few years now."

"What about right now?"

"Right now, I'm feeling like a teenager. Do you remember the tingling feeling you'd get when your crush would walk by you in the hallway, or look your way?"

"I do. My crush is standing before me, and I'm feeling a tingling sensation looking at her."

'I knew exactly where that sensation was.'

"Nadia, I've traveled many places, and I've seen many world beauties, but none have measured up to you."

"What if it's just lust?"

"I'm definitely lusting you. But I'm also falling in love with you. When you know, you know," he said, towering over me.

I failed searching for the truth in his eyes. I stared into them and became blinded by a combination of lust, desire, and naivety—clinging to his every word. Believing they were gospel.

"Will you let me love you?" he asked, molding my chin with his fingers, and nibbling on my lips.

"Love me, or fuck me?" I sighed, desperately wanting his kisses to continue.

They did. Up and down my neck. He slipped his fingers between my breasts, and slowly unzipped my suit.

"Both." He groaned.

I went with it, ignoring my inner thoughts trying to convince me I was being a fool.

'It's too soon for this to be love. You would be insane to let this man fuck you after three days. This is why they call you Naive Nadia.'

I couldn't resist the physical desire exploding inside of me. I wanted him. Bad. Badly. Properly. Now.

I shuddered when he slid the straps of my jumpsuit down my shoulders, seducing me with his gaze. I'd been wet for him for a while now, but the touch of his hands stroking the top lining of my bra sent shockwaves to my center.

My senses heightened from his gentle touch—giving me the sensational healing of reiki, but not all the way there.

I took his hand and placed it over my racing heart so he could feel his effect on me.

He grinned, then asked in the most virile tone, "May I touch you?"

"Yes," I answered in a delicate whisper.

Foreplay wasn't needed. I was heavily lubricated, melting from his grasp. The hook of my bra unfastened. He stood back and waited for it to fall to the floor, gave me a once over, then curved the side of his mouth.

My titties were on display for him to study every inch of my topless body.

"I'm going to remove those now." He pointed to my tangas.

"Okay." I sighed, panting hard as he stepped back towards me.

Mash fell to his knees, slid his fingers between my hips,

pulled my panties to my feet, and examined me. But this time, I was fully naked, trembling from his hungry breath warming the skin above my apex.

I gave him the power he craved. Idly standing by as he read me like a new book he hadn't opened.

He lifted my ankle. I quivered from anticipation, not knowing what to expect. Suddenly, his fingers traced my skin. They were warm, learning the curves of my buttocks until they reached my slick folds.

I crooned a light hum. Quickly, he pulled me closer to his face, and softly kissed my lower lips. I looked down. The bottom half of his face had become one with my thighs—his tongue enjoying the waters from the fountain between my legs.

"Aye, Papi," I muttered.

Mr. Sharper had my pussy pulsating and my tongue speaking in random Spanish.

I ran my fingers across his head while he held me in position. I balanced on one leg, then he placed the other across his shoulder. The maneuver intensified his tongue service, stimulating me to no end.

Lip service was something I didn't require, but occasionally enjoyed. I was quickly learning to appreciate it more, thanks to my oral specialist making me quaver from his skillset. This new lover of mine was undeniably experienced in tongue play.

He had to have sensed I was about to come. As soon as my body began to trill, he stuck his finger on my clitoris, and applied pressure, generously kissing me from my navel to my breasts with an open mouth.

He lingered between them for at least a minute, then sucked on my nipples while my body lost control in his grasp.

"You speak Spanish?" he asked, releasing his finger from my trigger spot.

"Not really," I answered with what little voice I could find. "I don't know where that came from."

He wiped his mouth with his shirt, then pulled it over his head. Not an inch of fat was on his abs. The black and brown stubble on his chest begged me to kiss them. So I did. Softly.

He flashed his whites at me. "I think you're ready for me."

He steered me towards the wall where he lifted my thighs with his wrists, and placed his wood against my crevice. I heard plastic crumbling. The smell of latex traveled up my nose when he drew back. He rolled the condom down until it smacked, and I exhaled with relief that we didn't have to have that talk.

'Fuck,' I thought, *'I didn't see what it looked like.'*

I'd never seen an ivory cock in person—only in bootlegged, x-rated videos. But I was about to feel one, and the lead up to that moment was too promising for it to be anything other than memorable.

My shoulders tensed, and I inhaled at the pressure from his first attempt to enter.

"Breathe," he commanded.

I didn't realize I was holding my breath. I let it out and opened my eyes.

"There you go." He slipped inside, coaching me as he saw fit. "You can take it. Good girl."

I gripped his dick inside my walls.

"Hold on to me." He warned, then fed me to the wall, leaving my imprint in the indigo cracks.

Back, forth, up, down, fast then slow, I was stroked without any struggle. With ease he lifted my body midair, moaning and complimenting how good I felt to him.

I held on for dear life, just as he instructed, tightly gripping my arms around his neck and shoulders. "Maximus. Maximus."

The sound of my voice made him thrust deeper. Then deeper. I was in mind-blowing ecstasy, taking a full beating, pinned between him and the wall with no way out. My heavily endowed lover was possibly ruining me, and I had no complaints. I loved it. Needed it. Savored every second of it. Rated it.

No one could top his performance and he knew it. He owned me. Staked his claim and planted his flag in my life box.

The more I pulsated on his dick, the less I became reserved. I pulled his head back to make eye contact. I had to look in the eyes of the man shifting my body into extremes.

He liked that I was finally engaging. Doing away with the shyness of it all.

"There she is," he whispered.

His coaching and talking me through it brought out an aggressive side. The more it grew, so did he. His moves switched to a slow grind with a sexy grin on his lips that told me to brace myself. This attentive motherfucker hit every corner he could find until I spasmed like my pussy was having a temper tantrum.

Our eyes connected as I arrived at orgasm number two. I rained on him like a downburst. He tightly squeezed me and amplified subtle, long strokes to apply the necessary pressure I needed to get it all out.

He removed his weapon. "You okay?" he asked, kissing my face.

"I'm more than okay." I whined. "Did you?"

He shook his head. "I'm not done with you yet." He swiftly kissed my lips, then led me to the pool table in the dining room.

I could barely lift my feet to follow him. Somehow, I managed to do so in my weak state. Was it hunger for more? The length of time since I was fucked senseless? Desire? Or him?

Not a whisper, command, or request parted his lips. He turned my back to him and positioned me up against the table, lifting one of my feet into the ball socket. His open mouth kissed the back of my neck until my back lowered and my breasts were on the green velvet.

A sudden insertion plunged into my warmth. I gasped, and screeched and grabbed on the table top, smiling below my hair blocking my face from his view.

I enjoyed him inside of me. Reveled in the sounds of his verbal expression.

"Nadia." He called me."You feel damn good, baby." He groaned. "I knew you would. I fuckin' knew it."

His dick relished my body. Helped itself to my juice. Found its home in my lines. And I in turn was pleased to receive all it had to give. The pain that paid off in pleasure. The sensation of sucks that led to fucks. All a lot to handle at first, but worth every second.

His hands massaged my back as he drove deep in my zone. Then he tugged on my hips when he thrusted side to side, enthralling me with levels of hedonism I never imagined—waxing my ass like he was the karate kid. Arching my back like it was a bow and his dick was the arrow.

A fist formed in my hair. He pulled it with half his strength to lift my head off the green velvet. He roared behind me like thunder, boisterously grunting as he let loose. I lied motionless during his release, squeezing my pussy tight around him until he howled like a lone wolf.

When he evacuated from between my legs, I lay lifeless at his mercy. He turned me around and I saw it. My God, I saw it. It was thickset and tawny, a lighter shade of brown at the base, and wider than I'd seen in real life. Absolutely perfect in my eyes.

I looked up at his face, then back at it once more— unable to look away from the culprit that just rocked my world.

"You made quite a mess," he said.

"I had some help."

He stepped backward into the kitchen and discarded the rubber. Then, grabbed two bottles of water from the fridge. Weak and disheveled, I stood in the dining room not knowing what to do with myself. He handed me a bottle of water, sat me on the edge of the table, then positioned himself between my legs. His hand caressed my back as I sipped from the bottle, wilted in his arms.

"Come. Let's take a shower and go to bed." He picked me up and carried me to the master bedroom.

"Awhew!" I shrieked, then rested my head on his shoulder.

He sat me down in the middle of a black, marbled double vanity. Steam rose from the running water as he called me over to join him.

"The master is nice," I said, rubbing soap across his back.

"The room or me?" He teased.

"Both." I teased back.

I was given privacy to cleanse the night off of me. When I turned off the shower, he met me at the door and wrapped a towel around me. On the bed, a t-shirt laid on a pillow with the sheets pulled back so I could climb right in.

While I bathed, Mash had taken the time to collect my clothing scattered all over the house. They were folded neatly on a chair at the foot of the bed, next to a tray with my water on it.

When he joined me, he sat up in bed, scrolling through his phone.

"Do you ever rest?" I asked him.

Buzz. My phone rang in my bag.

"Do you mind?" I asked him as if I needed permission.

We looked at each other, both confused by my question. I shook it off and answered Khai calling on Facetime.

"It's good to know you're okay," she said.

"I know. I know. I forgot to ping you." I stretched my bottom lip wide, then smiled.

"Why the hell are you smiling so big?" She laughed. " Are you lying down?" Her face got big on the phone. "And where is your make-up?"

"I only answered the phone so you could see I'm okay. I'll talk to you later."

"You better not hang up on me. Girl, you are glowing! Where is Mr. Maximus?!"

"He's right here."

"Hi Khai," Mash spoke from the background.

Khai cackled. "You are alright with me, Sir!"

"Girl, good night. Enjoy the room."

"I guess that means you aren't going with us to Paris in the morning?"

"No, I'll have to miss Paris. Bring me a chocolate croissant, please."

"I most definitely will. Talk with you tomorrow. Good night fornicators."

Mash replied, "Good night, Khai."

We laughed at the phone call then he took me in his arms.

"Are you cool with missing Paris to hang out with me?"

"Yeah. I wanted to go to Ibiza anyway, but that idea was thrown out the window."

"Ibiza? Why?"

"I'm fascinated with the big mythical rock, *Es Vedra*."

"I've had a few shows out there and never paid any attention to it. I've definitely heard about it, but my visits were mostly work, so my time there is always rushed."

"People say they can feel an energy from it. I was just curious to see it, and feel it for myself."

He kissed the back of my hand. "Well I'll make tomorrow worth your while since I'm interrupting your plans."

"You're a good interruption. I have no complaints."

"Check your phone."

A copy of his schedule for the week, highlighting the days and time he would be free during my visit was in my inbox.

"I have a show in Paris this Friday. Care to join me? It'll be my way of making it up to you."

"I can't miss the rehearsal dinner."

He snapped his fingers. "Just that quick, I forgot you're here for a wedding." He clicked his tongue. "Sooooo, I guess I'll see you sometime before, or after the wedding?"

"Wanna be my plus one?"

"I thought you'd never ask."

I give him a stern eye. "And you better not stand me up."

"Ha! She's bossing me already."

TASTE

4 a.m. I couldn't sleep. Under normal circumstances, I'd be knocked out cold after such an eventful week.

I was trapped under a hairy arm, unable to move. My eyes wandered from left to right, searching for clues and details Mash hadn't shared, or may have wanted to keep hidden—like a woman lived here with him, or he had a girlfriend out of town. Maybe even a wife somewhere.

Lying there I thought, *'Don't go down that road.'* But it was too late. The can of worms had been opened, and my mind wasn't to rest with those unanswered questions.

Since meeting him, everything had been too good to be true. And his house was too perfect for a woman not to be somewhere around. His room was well organized. Everything was in place in the kitchen, but he said he didn't use it. The pillows on the sofa were tucked correctly down the middle. And every bedroom smelled like expensive candles.

The marble abstract piece placed properly in the center of the nightstand next to a book and a lamp were all dust free. *'Maybe he has a maid,'* I convinced myself when my eyes grew heavy.

I closed my eyes and listened to Mash sleep peacefully next to me. I smiled thinking about how good I felt up pinned against the wall in the kitchen. Then, a record scratched in my head and images of other women in that same position made me cough.

Mash twisted from the sound and rolled over. Finally free of his arm holding me, I turned on my side, and tried to go to sleep.

He turned back around and slid closer to me. "Is something wrong?" his deep, groggy voice whispered in my ear.

"No," I lied. "How did you know I was awake?"

"I felt you move." He kissed the back of my head. "Are you comfortable?"

"On these soft sheets? Yeah, I'm good."

"Tell me what's on your mind?"

"Everything. Mainly the past three days, and how I ended up in your bed."

"You being in my bed isn't a bad thing, I hope?"

"It certainly doesn't feel like a bad thing."

His arm draped around my waist. He stretched the t-shirt he gave me at the collar and kissed the back of my shoulder.

"Then what's wrong?"

I sighed. "There lies the problem. Nothing is wrong. I'm trying to find something to be off, and I'm coming up empty. And Sunday will be here in a snap. And I have to get on the plane to go home."

"Kotch. Don't think about Sunday."

I snickered. "What does kotch mean?"

"Relax."

"I'd like to, but something else is bothering me. I wanna know who's gonna be in this spot when I leave? Yes. I know I sound jealous when I have no right to be. But I don't understand why you are single. I mean... Someone has to be keeping you company."

"If you're asking if I have a girlfriend, the answer is no. I have no reason to lie to you. Yes, I have a few friends I can call if I don't want to be alone, but nothing serious. Have I entertained them here? No. No one has been in this bed."

I turn around. "No offense, but I'm calling bullshit."

"I told you, I feel something for **you** that I haven't with anyone else. And I brought you into my personal space. I don't do that. Why are we talking about this?" He huffed.

"Because this is what I do. I overthink things, open my mouth, and everything goes to shit."

"I think you feel what I feel and you're scared. Admit it."

"I am a little scared."

"I have no intentions of hurting you. Do you believe me?"

I hesitated.

He pushed. "Say you believe me."

"I believe you."

"Now say you trust me."

"Nope."

He pressed firmly against my back, cocked and loaded, ready to strike. I'd been lying awake, waiting for a second round for at least an hour.

"Say it," he demanded, searching for my tickle spot.

"I said I believe you have no intentions of hurting me."

"Now say you trust me."

"Un uh." I screeched with laughter, until he silenced my giggles by sucking on my neck.

His tongue dragged across my skin. He bared some teeth and gently grazed the back of my shoulder, taking tiny bites that caused me to gasp.

I turned halfway to face him. "I trust you," I said, shocked at myself for uttering those words.

He smiled, then kissed me from my cheek to below my chin and back down my neck. "You don't have to worry about anyone else," he whispered softly.

He was convincing, but I didn't believe him. Fully. I wanted to, but my trust issues would always keep a small percentage of doubt around. That doubt would be challenged from a growing penis pressed against the back of my thighs. It made my pussy do *kegels*, and my body ready to wrinkle the sheets.

My legs spread open wide for him. Ready for the taking. To be visited by his thick member.

He palmed my bum, squeezing it like a stress ball as he grinded up against me. The t-shirt he gave me flew into the air, and I begged him to put it in.

He touched my warmth, then grinned at the drip coating his fingers.

"I want to feel the real you. May I?" he asked.

"Are you clean?"

"Yes. I always use condoms, but I want to feel you. The real you. Skin on skin."

I twisted, then looked in his eyes.

"You said you trust me."

I poked his chest. "Don't make me regret this."

"I promise, I won't." He instantly slid inside once given clearance.

"Ah!" I gasped, from the penetration.

"Breathe, my love."

His hands clenched my waist as he accelerated forward and thrusted all of him inside. He squeezed my body tight and groaned at the sensation of my pure flesh melding with his dick. He Grunted. Shrill cried. Moaned. Sighed.

The slow grind of push and pull ignited an awakening in me I couldn't fight. His voice, grunting against my chest somehow made me feel even closer to him.

Tighter and tighter, I cradled his head against me, rocking my hips back and forth in unison with his. He came up for air and I grazed my teeth against his shoulder. His head lifted and our lips met for a soft kiss.

"I love how I feel inside you," he whispered.

"I love how you feel inside me," I moaned.

"Woman, you are driving me insane."

He dove deeper, resting his lips on my forehead. He swept my hair off of my face, then tugged it from the nape.

"Iguh," I shrieked from the pull.

His eyes never left me as he watched me turn into putty in his hands. He pummeled the lower half of my body while simultaneously massaging my head until I drizzled on him.

He enhanced his strokes. "Messy girl," he taunted me with a wavering voice.

I screamed out, "Do whatever you want to me!"

That outburst swole his ego. He took it up a notch to next level shit, digging into me like crates as if he had been holding back all of this time. He concentrated on one of the toys he fancied in my box, and rung its bell so vigorously, he damn near wore out his welcome.

I placed a hand on his chest.

"Move that hand," he ordered, lifting my right leg and flipping me over while he was still inside.

I hollered. "Oh shit."

His hips crashed into my ass, thrashing me from behind. Lying flat on my stomach, I felt *ev-e-ry* inch of him against the back of my canal.

I had given him total control. Asked for it. Begged for it. My wish was his command and he initiated me into his world. And I loved it so much, I wanted to call it home.

He held me down by my shoulders, working me over, moving his dick in circles, pausing, then circling inside my pussy again.

"Baby, I'm close!" he shouted, "You're too much for me from the back!"

I clenched on the pillows. Body sprawled all over the bed. An animalistic bellow of delight, a howl of arrival echoed in the room as he climaxed.

His body fell on mine and he panted like he just completed a five mile run. Moments later, he smacked my ass and mumbled, "I wanna meet the bride and groom and thank them for bringing you to me."

We rolled to our side where I nestled next to him. I slipped my feet below his, and finally, rest found me.

♡ ✈

GOOD SLEEP DID my body good. At least the few hours next to a warm body saying all the right things, and applying pressure to the points of my body that needed it.

Some time after the sun rose, a presence stood above me. I opened my eyes to find Mash fully dressed.

"Sleep in. I have an errand to run."

"Leave some clean sheets," I muttered, then drifted back off.

By the time I fully rose, he hadn't returned. While he was gone I took another shower, brushed my teeth, and prepped my skin. I threw on the leggings and tee I hid in my bag, then snooped around his room to appease my curiosity.

At the foot of the bed were powder blue sheets. Next to them, a stack of photo albums Mash set out for my amusement. I snickered as I changed the bed, then made myself comfortable to fumble through the books.

The first one painted a colorful story of his teenage years. Photographs of him in a private school uniform, team sports, posing with album covers, and shadowing deejays filled in the first half. The second half displayed more moments of his early deejay interests—carrying crates of records, throwing up hand signs at parties, and what I assumed were old groupies or girl-friends taking to his shine.

The next book was family oriented. Old pictures black and

white portraits of beautiful people, which explained his striking looks. It dawned on me, we hadn't discussed our family history of where our ancestors hailed from as I turned the pages.

The book told me he was more than British. I made a mental note to bring it up in our conversation, if we experienced any lulls when he returned.

This third book was the most questionable, and impressive by far. A plethora of photographs with actors, athletes, singers, and models I recognized from runway shows, entertainment news, and my favorite shows.

Turning the pages wasn't good for my self confidence. Multiple, beautiful women smiled in pictures with him, playing with my insecurities like a fiddle. I began to imagine some of them lying on the bed staring at me, smirking and teasing that I didn't belong there. I slammed the book shut, envious of the women who made it into his memorabilia.

'Everyone has a past,' I said to myself, then snapped out of it as the garage door hurled and roared from the front of the house.

I rushed to the vanity to pull my hair back and fix my face. Mash walked in holding a small white paper bag in one hand, and shopping bags in the other.

His face curled as he glanced up and down at my attire. "You had clothes in your purse?" He laughed. "Someone wanted to spend the night, I see."

"And you are happy I did."

"I'm fucking ecstatic." He kissed me. "I bought you a few bits, but it looks like you don't need all of them." He dropped the shopping bags on the chair by the bed. "I'm sorry you missed Paris with your friends." He placed a pastry box in my hand.

A freshly baked chocolate croissant with two strawberries, soothed my morning hunger as I pulled the flaky pastry apart.

"As you can see, I was starving. Thank you," I said with a mouthful. "This tastes heavenly."

"Only the best for you."

I licked my lips. "Where are my manners? Do you want some?"

"No thanks. I'm enjoying watching you have a go at it."

"Good. Because I really didn't want to share it."

I closed my eyes and bit into the last piece of buttery chocolate bliss, savoring the flavors while wishing he had brought two of them home.

Licking the chocolate from my fingers, then chasing it with a strawberry, I pranced in my stance and nodded to Mash, motioning you did good. He turned the shopping bags upside down, covering the bed with new tags, a box of flats, and an array of panties and matching bras.

"How do you know these will fit?" I asked.

"For reference, I took pics of your labels with me to a boutique."

"Was this the errand you had to run this morning?"

"Sort of. Get dressed. We're going to be late if we don't leave soon. I'll wait for you downstairs."

"Late where?"

He trailed off and didn't answer. I found his assertiveness attractive, but stood there wondering if I'd given him too much control when I yelled, "Do whatever you want to me." I also wondered why I liked it so much. I may have been Naïve Nadia, but I'd never been so submissive that I did whatever I was told.

'Maybe he just wants to show me a good time while I'm here,' I thought, then popped the tags on a bohemian print skirt, solid magenta tee, and denim jacket.

I spruced up my make-up, threw on the flats, and accompanied my lover on a twenty-minute ride further into the country. We pulled into a private open-air field. One of my eyes jumped, and my heart raced faster than that plane sitting in front of me could run.

'Oh, Dear God! Please don't let this man think he is about to fly

me around in that thing. I'm already impressed! I'm already impressed!' I screamed in my head.

A short, elderly man appeared from the rear of a personal Beechcraft plane. "Park it over there!" he shouted, then tipped his hat.

Mash opened my door and I dragged myself out of the car. The older gentleman walked over and shook his hand, then reached for mine.

"Nice to meet you," he said, helping me out of the car.

"Nice to meet you."

"Nadia, meet Mr. Hunt, a longtime friend of the family."

My brows curved. "And a pilot I hope."

Mr. Hunt laughed. "For thirty years now."

I fanned myself and held my chest. "That eases my nerves."

Mash popped the trunk of his car and toted bags to the plane. The steps lowered. Mr. Hunt escorted me aboard, then briefed us with a tutorial on safety and emergency protocol.

"Where are we going?" I asked Maximus.

"Just trust me."

I gripped the edge of my seat at takeoff, counting the minutes until the plane settled in the air. Continuing to be tight-lipped about our destination, he dug into the bags he had hidden in the trunk, and passed a Sudoku book to me. The bag was filled with pencils, a mystery novel he hadn't finished, and a bag of chips—crisps he called them.

Mash gave me a cocky once over, then tapped my hand. "We'll be there in a few hours. Relax and enjoy the scenery. I've got you."

His poker face was stern as he circled words in the book. I stared at him thinking the croissant was a clue, and sat back in my seat, grinning that I had figured out he was taking me to Paris to meet up with my friends.

IN THE AIR

An hour into the flight I grew bored and anxious. I leaned over and helped solve a few puzzles, read some of his book, then asked him to give me a list of the songs he produced.

He pulled up his biggest hits, then we shared our playlists on our phones.

"I like your arrangement. You have open ears. You went from Kings of Leon to Nina Simone, Coldplay, OutKast, Prince, Edie Brickell, Fiona and Jay-Z in your shuffle file."

"Wait 'til you get to my Texas rap list."

"Why is it called Texas rap, and not just rap?"

"Because of how it sounds, and how it flows. They call it chopped and screwed. Stick with me kid, you'll learn something new." I clicked my tongue.

I played him a few songs from my favorite Houston artists. His reaction was priceless having never heard a record chopped and screwed before. I was giddy watching him take in the sound. His brows curved like he was studying the formula, and contemplating new ideas by the way his lips mouthed words to the tracks.

He removed his headset. "You have no idea what you just started."

"Glad to be of service." I pursed my lips and nodded. "I made the best CD mixes in college. Nobody could burn a better playlist than me."

"Will you make me one?"

"Let me guess. You still have a burner."

"Of course. It's all nostalgia in my profession."

"Speaking of your profession, I looked in your photo albums. How long have you been doing what you do?"

"For as long as I can remember."

"What was private school like?"

"Sometimes fun. Sometimes hectic. My mother is Italian and my father is full Brit. He raised me after they divorced. His claim was that he had the wealth and believed my mother couldn't teach me how to become a man, and being the one with the money, she couldn't fight him. He forced me to attend private school. Priding that I would be something great in his eyes. The next big thing if you will. And I was forced to try my hand in everything he deemed was great: Soccer, Lacrosse, Tennis, Rugby, Polo, Boxing.

'That explains his body.'

"Did you like any of those sports?"

"I was into boxing—up until I was knocked out. I continued training, but stopped sparring. Anyway, my interests didn't matter to my father. I was always attracted to music, but he didn't approve. I had to sneak around in clubs, and learn how to work turntables, speakers and mixing boards. Then, when I went off to university, I made a name for myself on campus."

"And look at you now. He must be proud."

"He wasn't around long enough to see me get to this level. He passed away."

"Sorry to hear that. My dad passed away three years ago. It's an experience you'll never get over."

"Losing someone you love, when the relationship was full of turmoil, is even worse. But you can't change a person, so it is what it is."

Maximus avoided looking at me. He stared out of the window, creating the lull I prepared for earlier, but we just discussed his mother's heritage, and a heartbreaking story about his parents' separation and upbringing. So, I let the silence last between us until he was ready to talk again, meeting eyes with Mr. Hunt watching us in his rearview mirror.

"There it is!" Mr. Hunt yelled.

I wobbled to the closest window, prepared to see the Eiffel Tower from the best view possible.

"What the!" I screeched, looking at miles and miles of turquoise water leading the way to the magical rock, *Es Vedra* in the distance. "You brought me to see the rock! I'm in Ibiza! The Baleares Islands of Spain! I can't fucking believe it!" I covered my mouth. "Excuse my language. Holy shit!" The glee I felt inside spread across my face. "I didn't think I was gonna see this place!"

"You were so close. And the way your face lit up talking about it, I figured I owed it to you...since you know...you missed Paris."

"I thought you were taking me to Paris to meet my friends. Ii assumed the croissant was a clue, but this is so much better! I can't believe you did this for me."

A black line dripped from the corner of my eye. I fought to hold my tears, but one resisted flowing back into my glands and dripped down my cheek.

"Come here." Mash reached for me.

I returned to my seat next to me.

Mr. Hunt cut in. "Buckle up, sweetheart. We are about to land."

My emotions were on overdrive. I couldn't resist kissing, necking, caressing and rubbing Mash as the plane prepared for landing. I didn't care that it was an inopportune time—Or that we had an audience. The only thing that stopped me from riding up my skirt to show my gratitude was the descent disturbing the moment. The drops forced me to compose myself.

"I can never repay you," I said.

"Your excitement is repayment enough." He kissed me one more time.

My feet touched the soil of Spain. My skin felt the breath of the calm water surrounding Es Vedra. My eyes magnified a landscape of beauty. My nose inhaled the scent of the crisp trees spritzed in the air before making it to the beach. I was already in love with the place.

We had four hours to tour. For starters, we shopped at the outposts we crossed. I found an array of organic oils and beauty products. Some of the brands were familiar. Several others gave promise, so I purchased them to test.

We taxied to the white sandy beach of Cala d'Hort, and dined at Restaurante Es Boldado. The mysterious rock *Es Vedra* sat beautifully in the view, making me anxious to take a stroll near the water before high tide.

As the sand on the beach invaded my sandals, I soaked in the energy of the magnetic rock I dreamed of visiting. Mash stood at my side, watching me take it all in: Meditating with my eyes closed, listening to the waves crash and burn, healing on the inside.

Its majestic presence was commanding. Everything I hoped it would be—calming yet thought provoking. Mystifying. Legendary. Wondrous. Extraordinary.

We wandered the beach until we reached the famous tower, Torre des Savinar. It was rumored to be the best place to witness the sunset, and from what we experienced, I concur.

The skyline melded from sapphire to bloodshot as the sun

slowly declined into the water, captivating us both. A peaceful-ness flowed within me. Mash held me from behind and draped his arms around me, gripping my waist, and stealing kisses on my neck. The burning ball in the navy sky began its journey to the other side of the world. As it traveled, a familiar feeling cloaked my chest. Fear struck a chord in me as I was too afraid to face what I knew had happened. I had fallen in love.

"Do you feel that?" he asked.

"I do. I can't explain it. It's so beautiful, and so, I, I…"

He pecked my cheek. "Sometimes there are no words."

But there were words. I just couldn't say them. I wanted to with every fiber in my body, but the idea of being silly, and my pride goading me to be cautious, I didn't…I couldn't be the first to say, " I love you."

My mind spoke for my heart. *Why does it matter who says it first? If it's real, it's real,* I thought.

Maximus chose action over words. He planted his saccha-rine lips on mine as a breeze of cool wind trapped us. Chills ran through my body. Wind flew up my skirt. The sun dipped while we spoke the words we refrained from saying, but expressed below the dark sky it abandoned.

Mash pulled back. "It's time to go home."

I smiled into his glimmering brown eyes. "I like the way that sounds."

A sly smile crossed his lips. "What do you like about it?"

"The home part," I said, then tasted his lips one more time.

✈

THE HOURS CREPT by slowly on the flight back to London. I had to fight off the urges to physically thank Mash with every restraint in my body.

Mr. Hunt delivered us safely to the London countryside.

Mash settled their business while I waited for him in the car. I watched his lips move as they talked. Arousal hit me hard, so I slipped off my panties before he made it to the car.

As he drove us back to his house, I brushed my hand through his hair, staring at him handle the curves of the road. When the path straightened, I took my panties out of my pocket, and dropped them in his lap.

He struggled to keep his eyes on the road when he asked, "When did you…?"

"Pull over," I said, unzipping his pants.

The car jerked to the side of the road near a dirt path that overgrown bushes masked as it led into the woods. Quickly, I surveyed the area for voyeurs with his wood standing at attention in my hand. I slid his trousers down a few inches, and marveled at its gloriousness.

It was the color of roasted red pepper hummus below the dim moonlight escaping through the clouds. Long in length, and wide like a mushroom at the tip, I saw why I was swooning.

My spontaneous gesture filled Mash with eagerness. He neglected to put the gear in park. The car rolled a few feet, and we chuckled as he shifted it in place, then turned off the engine.

I grabbed him by the face and kissed him, rubbing his glory with ease and precision. Enamored by his blessing, curiosity, arousal, and sensual stimulation made my pussy thump as he groaned.

"Allow me." I dove with a wet mouth.

He huffed at the touch of my slick and slippery jaws cupping him whole. As I took him in, he called my name.

"Nadia."

I increased the teasing, swirling circles around the tip with my tongue, then held his flinching head at the roof of my mouth. His moans deepened from the oral massage. I sped up the pace, making him jolt toward the pink of my throat. Up and down his bellend I sucked as he locked onto my hair.

Lower, my head dropped. Forward his dick advanced. I swallowed all of him, controlling my reflex, then slowly released him from my clutch.

"Fuck!" He cried out as I took a breather.

Like grinding fresh pepper, I rubbed him with tamed strokes. The look on his face sent me back down for more of a challenge, so I amplified my kisses to get the momentum going, then reduced the pace to slow soft licks.

He was triggered. His body slumped over in ecstasy.

"I love you," he whispered.

I rose when he said the words, lifted my skirt, and sprung on top of him. I screamed out from the painful delight of his insertion. I gripped on the headrest, remembering to breathe as his dick thrust upward.

He lent the assist, guiding my ass around his dick. "You look so beautiful fucking me."

I lowered to kiss him while matching his rhythm. The slow, deep strokes kneading my walls side to side had me wetter than the ocean we stuck our feet in hours before.

Mash reached for my face. I cradled his hand against my shoulder while he ran his other hand down my back.

Escaping my hold, he placed both hands behind my shoulders and locked me down on top of him. We locked eyes. Nothing but pure passion was between us.

"I love you, Nadia."

I grew weak and confessed. "I love you, too."

"Say it again."

"I love you."

His forehead pressed against my chest. "I loved you first," he whispered.

His deep voice in its sultry state made the words believable. The moment felt real. Felt right. Felt

Harder and faster my hips grinded around him. The motion drove him wild, producing steam between us. He spread my ass cheeks east and west. I squeezed my bum from the stretch. Heat fogged the cars windows. Sweat beaded between my breasts.

"Ah!" Mash gasped, holding me tight around his dick.

I rested my head on his shoulder, savoring the moment until I desperately needed air.

Beyond gratified, I returned to my seat. The engine revved.

Mash exhaled deeply. "Let's try this again." He grunted. "I need a smoke."

We didn't speak for the rest of the ride home. Long miles of silence had me worried I let the freak flag fly too soon. But damn, the man had literally charmed the pants off of me. Shopped for me. Flew me to Spain.

"I'm gonna hop in the shower," I said when we entered the house.

"You know where the towels are," he said, and went outside.

I watched him sit pensively by the pool, smoking a joint, staring at the water. After I couldn't watch anymore, I showered, put on one of his t-shirts, then scrolled my phone.

I looked at pictures of the girl's trip to Paris. I smirked, thinking about how I ended up going to Spain instead. I swiped and scrolled so long that I nearly nodded off waiting for Mash to come to bed.

Close to an hour later he popped in, took a shower, then did the same as me. He scrolled on his phone, but he was far away on his side of the bed.

The silence drove me insane. I lied there seething, and talking to myself in my head.

*'Say something. Anything. Please. What did I do to mess this up? You said you loved **me** for Christ's sake. Today was too perfect to end like this.'*

The past taught me not to react. To be patient. So, I did. But what I really wanted to do was cry.

I refrained from doing so out of pride. And so, I turned my back to him and tried to go to sleep.

I felt his eyes burning through me.

"Nadia."

"Yes."

"About today…"

"It's okay. You don't have to…"

"I don't know what I'm going to do when you leave on Sunday."

His tone was sweet and pierced through me. I turned around to face him, greeted by his solemn, handsome face.

"What do you mean?"

"I've been quite chuffed these past few days, Nadia. Sunday is fast approaching and I don't want you to leave."

"You do realize you haven't said a word to me in over an hour, and I've been over here trying to figure out what I did to ruin this perfect day we shared."

"I didn't mean to make you feel uncomfortable. I was just trying to come up with ways this could work for us."

"And."

"I just told you. I don't want you to leave." His hands ran across his mouth. "Today was one of the best days I've had in a long, long time. These past three days seemed like a dream."

I slid closer to him. "I feel the same way. How about we do as you said? Let's not think about Sunday."

I was relieved I kept quiet. A simple slip of the tongue and expression of rage over an hour of silence could have ruined everything.

His confession stunned me, more than his profession of love. He said it. I said it. But did we mean it? Truly?

We were somewhere on the borderline of love and lust. And having been addicted to someone physically before, I had to ask myself—Did I truly know how I was feeling?

The past seventy-two hours felt surreal. Love was here.

Looking me in the face, showing me what it was like to have it in my grasp. And I didn't know what to do with it because it happened so fast.

I had fallen. And hard.

HOSPITALITY

Travel began to wear on my body, and enigmatic pleasure added to my fatigue. Knowing Mash was concerned about a future with me eased my mind. It gave me confidence to relax in his home, and in his care.

I slept past midday, and probably would have slept a lot longer if I had placed my phone on silent. I had found a comfortable spot in the middle of the bed. The kind of comfort that once you lose it, there's no getting it back.

My phone disturbed the peace I was in, dinging back to back until I rolled over and checked my log. Khai called once, but the urgency of calls all belonged to Taylor.

I lied there with the phone in my hand, preparing myself for a one-sided conversation. I took a deep breath and dialed her number, regretting it the moment I pressed send.

"Hello, stranger," she answered.

I could hear rustling in the background, confirming she wasn't alone, and had placed me speaker. I took another deep breath, preparing myself for one of her performances.

"Stranger?" I frowned.

"I haven't seen you since Saturday. We were supposed to be

enjoying this trip together, as girlfriends. But *you* have run off with some random white boy that's got your nose wide open. What's going on with you?"

"Whoa," I said, not happy with her word choice or tone. "Let's back this train up. I'm not with a boy. I'm with a man. You didn't see me before I left on Sunday, because we were all taking it easy."

"Nadia, you missed going to Paris."

"So what? I told you I preferred going to Ibiza over Paris, remember? And going to Paris was optional. Why are you making a big deal about this? Do you need me for something?"

"Of course I do. You're here to be a bridesmaid. I can't believe you chose to lay up with a guy you just met, instead of going to Paris with your girls."

"I wasn't laid up yesterday."

"Then do tell. What did you do?"

"I went to Spain."

Taylor scoffed and laughed in her wicked way, mumbling with the phone muffled by her hand. A commotion of noise ensued in the background and I heard her faintly say, "This bitch said she went to Spain yesterday." Khai, Shannon, and Isla's voices became clear as they talked over one another.

"Nadia, everything is cool," said Khai. "What Taylor is failing to communicate, is that she feels you have forgotten why we are here. But don't worry, I think it's just a bridal moment."

Taylor shouted from a distance. "I'm not having a bridal moment! She is supposed to be here!"

"Excuse me, ladies," Mash interjected. "I apologize for yesterday. I told Nadia I wanted to meet the bride and groom, so would you and your mate have dinner with us tonight at my house?"

Khai whispered, "You should go. You need to do something outside of this anal retentive schedule you've created."

Her side of the call turned silent. I rolled my eyes. Mash bit on my arm. We laughed quietly, waiting for Taylor's theatrical performance.

"Mash, is it? Thank you for the invitation. But we don't know you, sir. Unlike the company you're keeping at the moment, I like to keep my word to people."

I cut her off. "Girl, just say yes already. You know you want to."

She huffed. "Well I guess my answer is yes then."

"I'll send a car," Mash added.

"We already have one."

"I'll text you the address. See you at seven," I said, then ended the call.

A POOL TABLE sat where a dinner table belonged. A highly critical and emotional guest was coming over, and dinner was to be served by my hands. With limited hours to prepare, the market run extended to multiple store runs. I was in search of foldout tables and chairs, a tablecloth, candles, vases, kitchenware and fresh flowers.

A pear and apple salad with a honey-lime vinaigrette chilled in the fridge, while my famous diced tomato short ribs, creamed potatoes, and sautéed spinach travelled through the house. For an added bonus, I baked Levi's favorite yellow cake topped with chocolate almond icing for dessert, and set it next to the floral centerpiece I arranged.

Taylor and Levi arrived on schedule. Mash welcomed them inside, and Taylor's eyes could not stop sizing him up. She became fixated with his hand around my waist, and hardly parted her lips, while Levi participated alone in the conversation.

"Why are we still standing here?" I asked. "Let's get some drinks in those hands."

As we walked to the living room, Mash thanked them for bringing me to London. Levi was his normal modest self, cool and collected, and dismissed the notion they had anything to do with fate.

Taylor, on the other hand, replied, "You're welcome."

I knew then we were in for a long night.

The men set off to smoke cigars in Mash's studio, while Taylor and I took a quick view of his house. Subtle sounds murmured behind me as she looked around each room, never offering a compliment.

When we made it to the kitchen, she stared at me as I fixed equal portions on the dinner plates.

"You seem right at home playing Suzy Homemaker." She shook her head and smirked.

I grinned. "I made the apple and pear salad you like."

"He seems to really like you."

"Taylor, I've never fallen for someone this fast before."

"Fallen as in Fell? For what exactly?"

"You know." I puckered my lips.

"You can't be serious." She laughed. "You two are so— different."

"Have you seen how fine he is?"

"He's okay, but still. He's... and you're..."

"Yeah, we are. And it doesn't matter. We click. I don't care about him being White. I see him as a person, and he makes me feel...well, he makes me feel damn good. I'm in love."

"Girl, stop playing." She fanned me off.

"You can judge me. Tease me. Do or say whatever you want. I've been bitten and I'm smitten."

"Okay calm down Foxy Brown. It's been what...four days?" She rolled her eyes.

"I know it sounds crazy, but it's true."

"Do you love him like you loved Dylan?"

"Dylan who?"

Taylor stood with her mouth slightly parted, and a look of disbelief on her face. Mash and Levi's voices grew closer. They entered the temporary dining room.

"Let's join our men," I said, snapping Taylor out of her zone.

She surprised me and carried the salad to the table. I trailed her with the dinner plates, happy to hear Mash and Levi getting on so well.

I considered Levi one of my male best friends. He was always a delight to be around. Most people saw him as a great role model for the youth, and he was patient, respectable, and reliable.

Being the great conversationalist he is, he kept the table talk interesting with discussions of business, sports, books, politics of the west, and entertainment knowing it was Mash's field.

"If you don't mind me asking, how much does all of that equipment run you?" Levi asked Mash.

"Quite a pretty penny. It's taken me years to get everything I needed for a fully functioning lab, but it was worth it. Studio time costs an arm and a leg. Now I can work from home and save my coins."

"You seem to be doing well for yourself— for a deejay," Taylor added.

Levi nudged her arm. Babe, that's inappropriate."

"It's okay." Mash sipped on some wine. "I do more than deejay at clubs and spin records. I do sound engineering, sound mixing, radio guest spots, and produce music. My next project is producing the score for a movie coming out this winter."

"By score you mean add the music to the scenes, right?" Levi asked.

"Yes. It will be a major accomplishment for me."

"Have we heard any of the music you produced in the U.S.?" Taylor asked.

"Probably not on the radio, but satellite radio spins them. Techno is bigger over here than it is in the States."

"It amazes me how different things are here. I can't get past the driving on the wrong side of the road," I said.

Levi, Mash and I laughed at my comment. Taylor stewed at how great we were getting along.

Mash shared a look with Levi. "You'll get used to it."

Levi chuckled. "Nadia, you did good with this one."

I nodded and rubbed the back of his neck, avoiding eye contact with the opposition across the table. Taylor rejoined the conversation, changing the subject to her wedding.

Mash didn't know Taylor well enough to know she was baiting him. Unaware of her trap, he thought it would be good to say something about the wedding to appease her.

"Is it okay if I come to the wedding as Nadia's plus one?" he asked.

"Weddings are for people you are close with. You know… family and friends. We don't know you like that."

Levi reached for her hand. "Don't listen to her man. Of course you're welcome." He turned toward her. "Baby, the man has invited us into his home. Don't be rude."

"That's the second time you've chastised me tonight."

Levi and I put our forks down knowing where the night was headed. We had years of experience with Taylor's flip side. Her ugly head had arrived, looking for a fight, and wouldn't stop until she got one.

"Am I the only person here who realizes how crazy you two are being?" Taylor's voice heightened. "Nadia, can you honestly say this isn't moving too fast?"

"I told you it was moving fast, and I'm on board. I'm happy."

Taylor pointed her fork toward Mash. "And you. Is this your first interracial relationship, Mash? What is your real name?"

"Wow. And no, it's not. My legal name is Maximus Sharper. Get it. Ma, Sh, Mash for short."

She scoffed. "You live half a day apart—by plane at that. How serious can you be with my friend?"

I tapped Mash on the leg and shook my head *no* so that he didn't answer her. I then shared a look with Levi before facing Taylor.

"Don't speak to him like that. He invited you here, and you're being beyond rude. What's up *witchu?*"

Taylor was blown away that I confronted her behavior.

She huffed. "This is all insane to me. You two are acting like you're so in love. You know nothing about each other."

"I know enough." Mash held my hand. "And I do love her."

"What?!" She exclaimed.

I lifted my head and shared a smile with him. He leaned over and kissed me gently, then looked at Taylor.

"And we don't owe anyone an explanation of what is happening between us."

She looked to Levi to speak on her behalf.

His hidden smile met her enraged gaze. "I'm not chastising you, Tay, but baby he's right."

Taylor threw her hands up. "Apparently, it's 3 to 1, so I'll go back to minding my business. I've said what needed to be said."

I took a deep breath. "Let's agree to disagree here. Everything is cool. When you bit my head off earlier, I assumed you were feeling like I was stealing your thunder. I promise you that is not my intent. I'm here for you. We just want to spend as much time together as we can before I leave."

Levi leaned toward Taylor. "Baby, apologize to them."

I patted her hand across the table. "No need. I know she's stressed out about the wedding. We're cool."

Levi exhaled. "Well I'm glad we got that cleared up, because I think I found my first bromance." He pounded fists with Mash. "Now can we cut this cake?"

HUMMUS

I laid naked in his arms, enjoying his strong hands caressing my back. My hands pressed against his firm chest as he stretched downward to kiss me.

"Morning," he said.

My eyes met his. "Five more minutes. Please."

"Then five more minutes it is."

The realization that we had to step outside of our bubble hit the next morning. I delayed returning to the city as long as I could, but it was inevitable as the hour quickly approached.

He walked me inside and we said our goodbyes. Pulling away from him at the elevator felt like watching him sail away on a Navy tour.

"Ring you later," he said, as the steel doors closed.

I reunited with Khai in my room, did a quick change into my purple Team Bride t-shirt while spilling the details about my escapades, and threw myself on the bed for the five minutes I had to spare until go time. I was back on the clock for Taylor, and she sure did know how to crack the whip.

That day, the weather in London was fickle. Sunny with wicked winds, making it chilly and warm one hour, then an overcast that came and went with a light drizzle that affected some of the planned games and family activities.

During the downtime, we stood around and gossiped. The constant stop and go killed most of the competitions, and when the sky turned completely gray, purple versus green ended earlier than scheduled.

Requesting that we move lunch up an hour early, some of the bridesmaids improvised with a talent challenge to kill time. Each family selected their best singer to compete, then forced the younger children to entertain everyone. Each side fought one another for the microphone, which helped as a distraction while we ran around like chickens with our heads cut off to serve the food.

Like good worker bees, the wedding party saw that everyone was fed before ourselves. With that checked off the list, the bridal party was finally allowed to clock out.

We gathered at our assigned table a few feet shy from the elderly section. The girls hadn't shared Taylor's bitterness with me to the entire party. Her cousin, Janine, unknowingly brought up my absence.

"Where have you been?" she asked.

"Around."

"I haven't seen you. I thought you were sick, or jet lagged or something when you didn't come with us to Paris."

Isla blabbed. "She was in Spain."

"I didn't know we had the option to choose where we wanted to go," said Janine.

"We didn't," said Isla. "Nadia, did you and Taylor work everything out?"

"Yup. We had a good time last night."

Janine smirked. "Work what out? Was there drama?"

Shannon cut in. "No. There wasn't any drama." She turned to me. "But since everything is cool now, tell me *fren*, what's it like being with a white man?"

Janine clapped her hands. "So, it was you they were whispering about."

My brows curved. "They were whispering about me?"

"It wasn't like that," said Khai. "When we went to Paris, Taylor was upset when she found out why you weren't there is all. They may have overheard a thing or two, but it's nothing to fret about."

Shannon added, "You know Khai wouldn't lie to you. Now that that's squared away. Give us the *deets*, girl."

"My lips are sealed. Don't ask me anything about the past couple of days."

"Then tell us about the nights." Shannon rolled her hips in her seat. "Come on, Nadia. You've been gone for like three days. If it was whack, you wouldn't have stayed over there so long. Now quit playing and give me something. You got down with the swirl, now tell your girl."

I frowned. "Why do you think I fucked him?"

Shannon's nose flared. "Cause you did. Is that rumor true that London men are the worst lovers?"

My lips parted. "No comment."

"I know you did it. From now on Nadia, I'm calling you GK. Grandma Klump. *"That's the only white man make me moist!"* Shannon quoted in the voice of the famous character.

The entire table burst into laughter, familiar with the scene from *The Nutty Professor* movie. I cried with laughter at Shannon's uncanny delivery of the line.

"Do not call me that!" I said, wiping my eyes.

Shannon tapped my arm. "I hear you. But he is a hottie. I know that much?"

I scowled. "How do you know?"

"I looked him up online. Hell, everyone's met him except me."

Janine slid next to Shannon. "Pull up his picture. I wanna see him, too."

Khai snitched. "Shannon did more than look up his picture."

"He is a celebrity. They always put their personal information out there. What people make per movie, net worth, etc. You're in good hands, girl." Shannon signaled ok with her fingers, then pulled up Mash's picture. "Ain't he cute?"

Janine looked at the image, then looked at me. "I see why you've been missing in action. I'd ride up to his house butt naked on a horse covered in honey."

Her comment exploded the table with more laughs. Few had to gasp for air. Others searched for napkins to wipe their eyes, and the elders at the table nearby laughed with us—except for Isla.

"What is your problem?" Shannon asked her.

"Why do you think I have a problem?"

"Because that was funny, and you are over there all stoned face."

Isla folded her arms. "It wasn't that funny."

"Don't worry about her, Shannon, her beef is with me. She called dibs on my guy the night we met, which is ridiculous."

Khai nudged her shoulder. "Is that why you've been starting shit? I peeped you being all in Taylor's ear. Not cool."

Shannon added, "Isla, how do you call dibs on a man? Please, do tell."

The table filled with snickers and all eyes shifted in Isla's direction.

"If you all will excuse me," she said.

The attention shifted back to me. Shannon continued her line of questioning, begging for details about my sexual conquest, and the appearance of my lover's lumber. I refused to answer her, but she wouldn't take no for an answer.

"I just wanna know if white men look like black men down there. You know, like how you can be with a light skinned dude, but his thing will be brown, or you can be with a dark-skinned dude, and his thing will be reddish looking, or..."

Khai cut her off. "We get the picture, Shannon."

"Seriously, what color is it? Inquiring minds wanna know."

Janine spoke out of turn. "*I'mma* say hummus."

"Hummus?" Shannon choked. "Hummus tastes just like it sounds—Hum-Ass."

For a brief moment, the table paused in silence. A mixture of chuckles and images of Janine's description pictured in our heads. We all looked at each other, guilty and tickled. Several hmm's and huh's collectively exhaled, then everyone burst into loud cackles.

The stir caught Taylor's attention. She moseyed over with Isla at her side.

"Y'all better not be over here laughing at me."

"We're not." Khai assured her.

"What's so funny?"

"Shannon," everyone said.

Shannon held up her hands. "I promise, I'm behaving."

"Then tell me what y'all laughing at."

Janine took the bait. "You came over just in time before I asked everyone a question. Who could be the vanilla in your sundae?"

Taylor pointed to the elderly table. "You do realize our grandmother is sitting right there?"

Shannon joked. "Grandma might have a story she wants to share."

"If she doesn't, I do!" The grandmother's sister shouted.

Shannon and Taylor's great-aunt snapped their fingers at one another, then shared a head nod of solidarity.

"See." Shannon pointed. "She knows what's up. Now let's see if it runs in the family. Who's on your list?"

Taylor sighed, then whispered, "Nick Jonas."

"Is he legal?" asked Isla.

"If he isn't, he will be when I'm done with him."

Khai huffed. "Yeah, let's hurry up and get you married."

"I'd do Brad Pitt," said Shannon.

Janine immediately jumped in. "Did you see him in Snatch?"

"Hell yeah. The scene when they burned his mama's van is why he's on my list. Come to think of it. He was smoking in Mr. & Mrs. Smith, too." Shannon and Janine high-fived, then she asked her. "Since you've already dipped your toes in the clear ocean, would you do it again?"

"Most definitely," said Janine. "Seth motherfucking Rogen."

Shannon nodded in solidarity. "I can see that."

Janine continued. "He's like a total package for me. Funny, cute, high all the time, cool, and a head full of curly hair. Hell to the yeah I'd smash."

Khai confessed. "I've always thought Thor looked like he packed a punch."

Shannon shook her head. "He was wearing a piece in Vacation. It was **not** real."

"How do you know that?"

"I researched it."

Khai scoffed. "Well he's still my pick."

"And a damn good one." The table moaned.

"Don't leave out Captain America either," Janine added.

"Yeah, he's very seasoned." Shannon fanned herself. "What about you, Isla?"

"I support black love. I've never given it much thought." She turned up her lips.

Taylor looked at her with a side-eye. "You told me you would fuck Jon Snow!"

"I told you that in confidence!"

Khai chortled. "Like you would ever meet him."

"Jon Snow and Daario Naharis." I cosigned.

Isla sneered. "Which Daario?"

"The first one."

"Yes *Lawd*. That Daenerys is a lucky bitch."

Shannon's eyes narrowed. "Who the hell are y'all talking about?"

My voice and Isla's synchronized. "It's a Game of Thrones thing."

"Why are we talking about this again?" asked Taylor.

Isla sighed. "You know why."

"Pardon me, ladies." Levi pulled Taylor away.

We looked on at what appeared to be a serious chat with hand gestures, pouting, and pleading. Taylor returned to the table, gave me a dirty look, then accused Mash of being a troublemaker.

"Your little friend has invited Levi and his groomsmen on a party bus with strippers tonight."

"Can I go?" Shannon asked.

"What's wrong with that?" I asked.

Taylor's turned red. "Call him and tell him to rescind his offer."

Under severe scrutiny, I dialed him. *Don't answer,* I sang to myself as the line rang. Unfortunately, he picked up. Heavy music blasted through the phone. No greeting—just vibrating bass and chatter in the background.

"Sorry about that, love. I wasn't at a stopping point. Is everything okay?" Mash asked.

"Not really. Taylor would like to have a word with you."

Taylor swiped my phone from my hands. "Levi already has a bachelor's night planned. He doesn't need your party bus."

"If it's a problem, you're welcome to join us."

Shannon bounced in her seat. "Say yes. Say yes. We all wanna go."

"How many people can this bus hold?"

"It's a party bus. However many we want."

"And how well do you know these strippers? In fact, who are these people coming with you?"

"I'm bringing the artist I'm working with at the moment. Whom I need to get back to."

"Fine." Taylor huffed. "Expect all of us tonight. We're crashing the party."

I gave her a death stare as she handed me the phone.

"Sorry to bother you with all of this," I said to Mash.

"Everything's fine. See you tonight."

Across the room, I locked eyes with Levi being confronted by Taylor. He shook his head in disappointment. A look of defeat across his face.

I mouthed. "Sorry," containing my anger toward Taylor's behavior.

SHOTS

To avoid further conflict with Taylor, I skipped the group sauna session. I hadn't had a moment to myself in days, so while Khai was busy taking advantage of the hotel amenities, I hung back in the room for some me time.

I showered, threw on my pajamas, pulled out my tablet, and fell asleep before tapping a key.

When it was time to infiltrate the party bus, Mash texted:

> Come to room 414.

He greeted me wearing a towel around his waist, seducing me with his smile. "You know we don't have time for this," I said, stripping him bare. He chased me around the room, begging for a quickie, but pleasure had to wait.

A cloud of smoke floated from the doors of the bus when it rolled into the lot. The recording artist and his entourage claimed the seats in the rear before we boarded. The strippers greeted everyone with poses on the poles, and we joined a party that started without us.

The wheels set in motion. Acquaintances were made. The men crowded the back of the bus partaking in weed, cigars, and liquor. The women loosened up with the help of the strippers that forced us to dance with them. An exchange of moves were shared from both sides, then we blended when the hit song mixed in.

All of the bridesmaids jumped up and shouted, *"I get it how I live it!"* The bus bounced and we went into a frenzy. The floor of the bus vibrated. The driver's assistant peeped at us through the curtain.

Harv Legend, the artist onboard, came from the back of the bus and groped my legs. I brushed his hands off of me, then made my way towards Mash.

I continued my dance in front of him. He blew smoke in the air and grinned at me. Harv's eyes followed my every move. Mash signaled, *she's with me,* with a hand gesture.

Harv asked. "Is this wifey you were banging about?"

Mash nodded.

"Man's not foul." Harv held up his hands.

I toned down the dancing. The ganja flowing freely had given me a contact high. The grope made me feel uncomfortable to wind how I normally would. Also, the sexy smoldering way Mash looked when he lowered his bottom lip to the side to exhale a cloud of smoke also turned me on. I sat in his lap and kissed him.

He whispered in my ear. "Don't do me like that after you denied me in the room."

"You miss me, huh?"

"It's why I got us a room. You look sexy tonight. I love seeing you so carefree like this. Reminds me of the night we met."

"And you look handsome as always. Who taught you how to dress?"

"I put my garms together."

"Your friend keeps looking at us."

"He's harmless. My fam. Forget about him. I'm more concerned with getting you out of these jeans you have painted on. I can't wait to get you home tonight."

"You mean the room?"

"Wherever you and I are together is home for me."

I squirmed. "I just got a little wet."

"Naughty Nadia. I might have to bend you over in an alley somewhere. All of this teasing, I should warn you. There will be no love making tonight. *Capiche?* Think you can handle it?"

"I know I can handle it."

Bar one interrupted our provocative moment. The crew went inside, enjoyed a few rounds at the bar, and took over the mucky, minuscule dance floor. Mash and I creeped to a dark corner and made out under a dart board. The way he felt pressed against me ignited a fire in my jeans. It reminded me of my high school days, when I allowed my first boyfriend to hunch on me for five minutes against the wall at the dance.

I chuckled in Mash's ear. "Last time I did this, my boyfriend left me for a girl who actually put out."

He growled. "Tonight, I'm that boyfriend and you're the girl that's putting out."

The urges burst through me like flames. I throbbed uncontrollably in my jeans.

"Posse out!" Levi shouted.

Our party scattered back to the bus. The girls pulled me away from Mash, teasing me about our antics at the bar.

Harv sat next to Mash. The bass in their voices carried over the music. I overheard their conversation with my back toward them. And I didn't like it.

Harv asked, "How in the hell did you pull her?"

"I got lucky," Mash answered him modestly.

"The bird is bad. She could have easily been mine if I saw her first."

"Maybe. But I saw her first and here we are."

"Don't switch. Man's not on the defense. Easy."

"We safe."

Their slang was hard to follow. It was choppy and proper—also confusing at times because of enunciation. I didn't understand everything they said, but I got the gist of it. I hoped Mash was right that his friend was harmless, and plotted to put one of the girls on him. I prayed he would take an interest in someone else.

I observed our group closely, searching for a good match for the rapper. We arrived at Bar 2 before I could make my pick.

Half of the bus went inside. The other half continued to dance in the aisle and on the poles. Mash and I stayed behind on the bus, contemplating the safety of a quickie in the alley behind the bar.

The absurdity of it made us laugh. So, we agreed to distance ourselves to cool off. He would stay with the fellas, and I with the girls. But Mr. Sharper didn't make our separation easy. His lingering eyes watching my every move made my chest ache to be near him. By the time we reached bar 3, his words were all I could think of. *"There will be no love making tonight."* I couldn't help but focus on what he meant by that as I stared at him across the room.

Bar 3 was cleaner than the first two stops. My boots didn't stick to the floor, and the wood on the bar shined. Bar 4 was within walking distance. Like kids on a field trip, our party took a short stroll to the bigger establishment with a crowd standing out front.

The girls and I recognized that the strip resembled uptown back home. A tightness surrounded my heart at that moment. I looked back at Mash having a good time with Levi before we entered. Immediately, I thought about Sunday approaching and wondered, *'How am I gonna leave this man?'*

The bridal party occupied the bar. I ordered a fuzzy navel on the rocks, drank it like a shot, then followed with a sex on the beach. Shannon ordered a triple basket of lemon pepper wings and fries. She harassed the bartender to speak with the chef so she could tell him how to make them wet with butter.

"Don't mind her," Khai said to the bartender. "She's had one too many."

The men crowded Levi at the opposite end. Huddled together like frat boys, they chanted, "Cheers! Cheers!," and threw back shots.

"One more round!" yelled a groomsman.

The wings arrived and it was every man for himself. It was the first time any of us had been silent since boarding the bus. The groom party ordered two dozen more for the road. While we waited, we danced with the locals, creating a Soul Train line to show them how we get down back home.

One by one, we called each other's names to show off their moves. A crowd formed around us, pushing us too close to keep it going. A hand wrapped around my waist.

"It's time to go," Mash said.

"Next!" yelled a groomsman, and we bolted like Usain.

At the last stop of the night, the entire party huddled at the bar doing shots.

"On the count of three!" yelled Janine.

A collective gasp by those chugging with no chaser, ended the night.

"I'm getting married!" Levi shouted, then kissed Taylor.

We surrounded the bride and groom with hugs and cheers, then filled the small dance floor. Bridesmaids danced with groomsmen, and sometimes with Mash's friends. It got wild with two on one at times, and that's when I sat down at the bar, pretending not to notice Harv looking at me from one side of the room, and Mash eye fucking me from the other.

Half of the bus was faded on the way back to the hotel. The other half learned pole tricks from the strippers. Those that were coupled up watched the action.

Smoke veiled the bus when we parked in The Mandarin's lot. Passengers trickled out at their leisure. I left when Mash looked my way with pure lust in his eyes. He took my hand and we hopped out without saying a word to anyone or each other.

Like sex crazed maniacs with no regard for elevator etiquette, we started on each other with a passenger in front of us. The heat between us could have warmed an entire floor. Buttons were broken. Jackets were stripped. My hands rubbed his chest beneath his shirt. His mouth was damn near down my blouse.

He chased me down the hall. I pressed against the door making him kiss me to move so he could swipe the door with the key. We stumbled inside our suite. He tore what remained of my top as we headed for the bed.

"I'll buy you a new one." He sucked the air from my mouth.

My jeans were the only thing in our way from touching skin. I was hard-pressed against the linens with a pulsing pussy begging for punishment.

Mash unzipped my boots and aggressively slid my jeans down my legs. He stared at me with a beguiled face. Heavily, I breathed, wishing I could read his mind. To compare what he was thinking with what his eyes were saying.

He reached for the floor and held up my boots, then zipped them back on my feet.

"Dance for me," he ordered, in a masterful tone.

I took my time getting into a slow rhythm up against him, swaying in the silence. I became his private dancer. His personal one woman show.

First, I rubbed my ass against him, then turned around and dropped to my knees. I untied his boots, then dragged my face up his body. My finger pressed against his chest, guiding him to the chair next to the bar. I leaned in like I was going to kiss him, but stopped short and nudged him 'til he fell back into the chair.

I sauntered to the bar and poured him a swig. I served him

the first sip, tipping the glass just enough for a drop to coat his throat.

He took the glass from my hand. His fingers took their time trailing away from mine. When they no longer touched, I floated across the room.

My phone was still in my jacket. I pulled it out and selected Paula Cole's *'Feeling Love'* from my mood playlist to set the tone. The beat was perfect to match the way I swayed my hips. Her high pitched vocals began at the perfect time for me to rub my hands across every sensuous zone of my body.

Mash adjusted himself in the chair with a bulge protruding the front of his denim. I eased over and freed him. Teasing him with slow strokes up and down his shaft, then backed away, rolling my body slowly.

His eyes never left the red lace clinging to my dewy skin. I placed my pussy on the sheets and hunched the bed, then playfully tapped my ass cheeks. Gentle at first. Slightly harder for the second. Then hard enough to make a *smack* sound.

Mash grabbed his pipe. I turned over to my back and kicked high to the ceiling, pointing my heels above my head. The move reeled him over to me.

I rolled to my knees and posed with my back arched, tossing my hair like a wild cat. Mash grabbed a patch of it. He lowered his face to mine and roughly kissed me with a tongue that tasted of pure vodka and whiskey.

"Remember what I said earlier. There will be no love making tonight," he whispered in my ear.

I nodded.

He let go of my hair, flipped me over on my back, and spread my legs wider than the floor plan of his house. He sucked my vulva hard above my lace thongs. "Someone couldn't contain themselves." He groaned, then frayed them in half with a strong tug. "I'll replace these too."

There was nothing gentle, or soft about his kisses to my

pussy. He feasted on me violently with fast, wet licks and vigorous suction and cupping.

I panted and moaned as I pulled off his shirt in the midst of him making a meal out of me. Once it was in my hands, I muted my cries with it.

Mash removed it from my mouth. "I want to hear you taking this dick."

He tossed it to the floor, then held down my hands. They rested at my side while he gazed into my eyes, then a sudden hard invasion split my core.

This time he wasn't gentle. This time he didn't tell me to breathe. I gasped at his insertion, sprinkling on him from initial penetration. He tongued me hard, moving my hands from my waist side to above my head. He restricted them, intertwined with his to forbid me from holding him back.

He had kept his word. There was no love making between us. This was a strict fucking and exploration of my walls. A test to see how much dick I could take. How rough I could tolerate him. How long I could last under these conditions.

There was no remorse in his strokes. No regret in his poaching. No shame in the sounds he made. No letting up on his attack.

The friction and the motion forced my boots to meet my confined hands above my head. Mash continuously and ruthlessly pounded me into the springs of the bed, then finally kissed me softly as he neared his end.

Suppressed beneath my punisher pummeling pure joy from my pussy, I was locked in. He had us pinned together as one body. One entity. I couldn't stop him if I tried, and I didn't want to. I was tipsy, tired, and taking it.

"Papi, Papi, Papi!" I screamed to the heavens.

Mash shuddered and opened fire. "I'm about to shoot to the moon!"

His body grew tight and strong, as he squeezed me in the

strenuous position, bucked to the Gods. One hand rose to my neck and clasped around it. The force cut off my oxygen as I came with him, leaving me wounded. Winded. Breathless. Complete.

"I love you," he said, and fell to my side.

GOODBYE

We had to say goodbye again. Underneath the loading zone, Mash left me behind for Paris. I entered the revolving door, looking back for his silhouette through the glass. But he was gone, leaving behind the delightful damage he'd done to my body the night before.

When I made it back to the room, he texted:

I won't be like that always.

A good manhandling is alright every now and then.

I wondered if he noticed a difference in my walk the next morning, or did I not manage the rough ride to his liking. Nevertheless, it happened and would hold me over until I saw him again.

In the meantime, I was occupied with responsibilities that began in the Shoreditch district of London. The schedule called for shopping and wedding look run-throughs for Taylor to approve.

I wasn't physically fit for hours of running around after I'd been smashed to smithereens, but to keep the bride happy, I hung in there as best as I could.

Hours later, the spa at the hotel welcomed us for manicures, pedicures, and hair trials. One by one we rotated between each station with complimentary Rosé, Pinot, and Sparkling Wine.

Taylor's bridal package didn't include full service amenities. Once my hands and feet were painted, I treated myself to a deep tissue massage and facial, and charged it to room 414.

The bridesmaids toasted Taylor when the final pedicure was complete.

Janine raised her glass. "To Taylor, our beautiful bride. The reason we're here on this memorable getaway."

"To Taylor!" We toasted.

"Cousin, if it weren't for you, I'd never have come here. And you kept your word that this trip would be a week-long event of fun and good times. Thanks for letting me be a part of it," Janine added.

"And thank God we don't have hideous dresses." Shannon raised her glass.

"I wouldn't do that to you guys. What do I look like having ugly dresses in my photos."

Janine chimed in again. "And thank you for making the grooms let us tag along last night! I had a damn ball."

"We did have a good time. Didn't we?" Taylor looked at me cross. "Aren't all of you glad I spoke up?"

Shannon faked a cough. "Here, here. I was so messed up, I hooked up with one of Levi's cousins. And I can't remember his name."

Taylor frowned. "Shannon?"

Shannon waved her off. "I'll point him out at rehearsal."

Khai shook her head. "That's a damn shame."

"She's not the only one. Right, Janine?" Miri, Janine's younger sister shared.

"Stop telling my business."

Miri sucked her teeth. "Which reminds me, does anyone want to trade roommates? Because mine brings home random men in the middle of the night."

Taylor cut in. "Who did you hook up with, Janine?"

Janine lowered her head. "The rapper guy."

Shannon shamed her. "He was trying to get at everybody. Why did you let him hit?"

"I was messed up. And his team was doing a party pack in the back of the bus, so I might have accidentally taken a molly, or X, and got serviced. It's no big deal. It ain't like I'm catching feelings or nothing."

Miri rolled her eyes. "They sounded like animals in the bathroom. I had to put a pillow over my head. No one wants to hear their sister getting it in."

Taylor quieted the room. "Okay. That's it. From here on out, no one is to hook up with anyone else. Got it?"

The room snickered.

Shannon raised her hand. "Excuse me, General Tay. You can only babysit one punani—Yours."

Everyone including the service team cried with laughter.

✈

I CLOCKED out for the night and returned to 414 for some R&R. To wind down, I attempted to get some writing done. I sat against the headboard, reflecting on the past few days. There was so much to journal that I didn't know where to begin. Flashes of the club, the dance battle, the first, second, and third kisses, the romantic stroll in the city, the sex, the plane, the rock, the sunset, sex, sex, the couple dinner, the bar crawl, and the room I sat in.

I stared at the blank page with my hand on the keys, but all I wrote was, '*2 days until I see him again*'.

Thinking about where to begin, I procrastinated further and

read my emails, sorted my receipts, and organized my luggage to make everything fit. A wave came over me when I picked up the ripped thong. I climbed back on the bed and outlined my week, starting at the beginning, and chuckled when I proofed it and saw how many times I wrote the word sex.

Thirty minutes later, my journal had turned into a first chapter draft. I blushed at our story, and closed my computer. My hands crept in between my legs pressed together. I held myself to savor the feeling from last night, and dozed off in a fetal position.

The room phone startled me when it rang. It was the day before the wedding. I started the day with the recorded voice waking me and sighed. I wanted to lie in bed all day, but duty called with one last hurdle before the main event—the rehearsal dinner.

My assignment was to oversee the decor. To make sure the correct amount of roses arrived, that they were tied correctly around the podiums, and aisle. That the reception tables looked identical to what Taylor selected out of the magazine. And be the second pair of eyes on the programs when they were delivered.

My tasks were easy compared to the others in charge of treating Taylor like royalty, which was why she chose to marry in England. They rotated shifts in catering to her every need, ironing her clothes, helping her remain calm, and listening to her bitch and moan.

Levi's grooms relaxed while the bridesmaids ran around like chickens with their heads cut off for the second time on the trip. Happy hour even began early for them. By the time we showed up for the rehearsal dinner, their eyes were already glossy and red.

The vibe was stressful, beautiful nonetheless, and full of emotions running wild. Taylor cried so much it became contagious. When we lined up she was in tears. When Isla and Drew, the best man, walked in the bride and groom's place, she wept. Then Levi cried. So Isla cried. By the time we were done, a wave of tears had taken over the room.

Afterward, we all appeared to be composed in the banquet hall. The drink flowed. Conversation remained positive. And the bride kept it together until their family and friends sang praises of the happy couple.

Dinner was served. A few of the grooms were looking for more than food to be on the menu. I excused myself while everyone mingled to answer a call. When I returned, I over-heard Isla discussing me with Taylor and Janine.

I fumed listening to them ridicule my behavior. I knew Isla was jealous, but I thought she had gotten over it since game day. I waited a few seconds before walking up on them and pretended that I hadn't heard a word to watch them squirm.

"Where are you coming from?" Taylor asked.

"I had to take a call. What's I miss?" I asked.

"Nothing," said Isla. "Just making sure the bride is happy with the way things are going."

"Are you?" I swallowed hard to play their game.

Taylor smiled. "No complaints. Just a few more hours and I can finally exhale."

I looked at the time. "Well, we should be getting some beauty rest. I'm gonna turn in. See you all in the morning."

I walked away with my face balled up in a knot. Proud of myself for being the bigger person. I cried to myself in the room.

♡ ✈

A BRAID CROWNED the front of our hair. Loose wavy curls fell between each stitch. The bridal party circled Taylor in her room, perfecting her strands and her straps, and dressing her while she cried like a baby.

We prayed for a perfect day as her hands shook, and delayed the glam team to have her ready on time. Levi stood outside of her room. We were excused to give them a moment. Whatever he said gave her the push she needed to get the show on the road. Thirty minutes later, we preceded her down the aisle in our mint colored gowns and fuchsia flowers in hand.

The ceremony began with a solo from a member of Levi's family. Taylor's aunt read a poem after the song. The minister performed a lengthy service with a scripture reading, followed by a short story about the roles of a husband and the duties of a wife.

I searched the room for Mash, hoping to catch a glimpse of him since we barely spoke after he left. *'Where is he?'* I wondered, after scanning the crowd with no luck.

During the lighting of the unity candle, Taylor's waterworks returned. Levi wiped away her tears, but by then the room cried along with her. Including me.

My tears were a combination. I was happy for the couple, but sad for myself. I was moved by the ambiance of love in the room, while dreading that my time with Mash was ending. It didn't seem fair that the love I found was temporary, while theirs was permanent when the pastor pronounced them man and wife.

I wiped away the mess forming around my eyes for the million photographs we took around the property during cocktail hour. When we were done, I swore Mash would have arrived by then.

The reception was underway and there was still no sign of him. I searched every table for his face as the wedding party was introduced. I couldn't place him in the room. The couple's first dance came and went, then Taylor danced with her father. Levi followed with his mother, then mother-in-law, and the dance floor opened to everyone. My heart sank when I realized Mash was not coming.

It wasn't the way I would have said goodbye, but I understood the gift he was giving me. Our time would forever be cherished. I just wished I could feel his arms around me one more time. And if I had known our last kiss was the final time my lips would touch his, I would have held it a little longer.

Isla and Drew gave their speeches and toasts. I swallowed a glass of champagne on the sideline, watching my friends and both families dance.

Feeling bummed and burned, I lost all of my composure. I needed answers. I needed to get to my phone, which was forbidden during the ceremony.

I slipped out of the reception and went up to 414. I searched for something with his scent on it, but he'd packed all of his belongings when he left for France. The only thing remaining in the room with his aroma was the pillow he slept on. I held it in my arms, imprinting the notes of the cologne on my brain.

My phone had zero missed calls and one unopened text, but it wasn't from him. "You did this to yourself," I shouted across the room, paced back and forth in disbelief.

I was to blame for being a fool. Believing that love found me. Losing control. Ignoring my mind telling me not to buy into the fairytale. For listening to my heart.

A knock on the door disturbed my pity party. I ran to it, hoping I had worked myself up for nothing.

"Is everything okay?" Khai walked inside.

My mascara ran down my cheeks. "I'm such a fool." I cried.

She held my hand. "I watched you look for him all day. You're not a fool, honey."

"Then why isn't he here? He hasn't even called. Or texted."

Khai wrapped her arms around me, doing her best to console my aching heart. "What did he say the last time you spoke to him?"

"That he loved me and was coming to the wedding." I pulled away from her. " I mean I get it. Why prolong the inevitable when he was already free from me? Ya know? Why leave Paris and come back here when the hard part has already been done. He's not tied to me. He doesn't owe me anything."

"You're getting yourself all worked up. He wouldn't just ditch you like that. I saw you two together with my own eyes. He's crazy about you." She twisted her mouth. "Not to worry you, but maybe something happened. Like he missed his flight, or someone stole his phone so he couldn't call you. I'm sure he doesn't know your number by heart. No one knows anyone's number by heart." She grabbed a Kleenex from the box on the dresser. "Collect yourself. Okay? If you don't hear from him by tonight, then we can worry. But right now, you need to come downstairs and enjoy yourself. Let's get you cleaned up."

She wiped my dripping mascara, and touched up the red areas on my face. Once I was concealed with minimal red eyes you'd have to study me to see, we returned to the party.

I put on a mask and danced with a persistent groomsman. The one I noticed the night we arrived. I put up a good front until he danced a little too close. So close, I got a whiff of his cologne, and felt heat coming from his body.

I faked a cramp. "I've been on my feet too long. I need to sit for a moment." I limped to the closest chair, took off my heel, and rubbed my feet to sell my story.

Sitting there, I faked a smile with everyone that crossed me. When asked about my eyes, I used the wedding as an excuse.

"I cried with everyone else today. The ceremony was so beautiful," I said.

That lie worked, until simpering face Isla spotted me sitting alone. It was the moment she'd been waiting for all week. Her chance to humble me.

Tension ran down my spine just looking at her walk my way. I had to be strong. Not let her belittle me, or fall for the bait to rile me up. I preached to myself, *'Keep your cool. Don't give her the satisfaction.'*

"Where is Mister 1's and 2's? I haven't seen him around for a few days. Trouble in paradise already?"

I chuckled. "Humph. Mister 1's and 2's. That's cute. How long did it take for you to come up with that one?"

"I'm just teasing. But for real though, where is he? I thought Taylor said he was your plus one?"

"You and Taylor have been doing a lot of talking about me and my plus one. Why is that?"

"What do you mean?" She stuttered.

"I heard you last night. And I quote, "This weekend was supposed to be about you, and Nadia's been running around in la la land with her nose wide open over a fling." End quote. Sound familiar?"

"Did you seriously think it was something more? You're smarter than that. At least I thought you were."

"Isla, humor me. If he chose you that night, what would you have done?"

"Don't deflect. I was simply saying it was embarrassing how you were carrying on. But seeing as though he isn't here, I'm sure you've snapped back into reality. Sorry it didn't work out the way you wanted." She smirked.

"Now look who's deflecting. You didn't answer my question."

"You didn't answer mine. Do you know what your problem is, Nadia?"

"Her problem is she isn't dancing with me." Mash rubbed my shoulder.

I turned around.

"Sorry, I'm late." He reached for my hand. "I thought I'd catch you out-dancing everyone." He smiled.

He wore a tailored tan suit accentuating his broad shoulders, and a powder blue oxford shirt and tie to match. I rose to my feet, hiding my face from him as he escorted me to the dance floor.

I followed his lead. "Do you know what you're doing, captain. This is a fast song."

"Let's pretend it's a slow one," he said, holding me close. "You look amazing by the way."

"You clean up well yourself. Very dapper look you got going on here."

He kissed my forehead. "Have you been crying?"

"Everyone cried today. I also had a slight meltdown, but I'm okay now."

"Why? What happened?"

"I didn't think I was gonna see you again."

He held me from the nape of my neck, and placed his head against mine. "You thought I ghosted you?"

I nodded.

"I would never do something like that to you. I had a few errands to run before leaving Paris. One was finding these two a wedding gift. Then of course, I had to get you something. I had to fight traffic, rush home to get dressed, get back in traffic, and time just wasn't on my side today. But I'm here now."

I closed my eyes. "Remember when I told you that I overanalyze everything? I thought you were making a clean break from me without all the drama."

"Look at me." He lifted my chin up. "I told you I love you. I also told you that I mean what I say, and I say what I mean. Never forget that."

"I love you, too."

"I would have called, but you told me you wouldn't have your phone at the wedding. You have no idea how gutted I've been these past two days. I've done nothing but dread tomorrow. I want you to stay."

The thought had crossed my mind. I didn't dare tell him that. Instead, I hugged him tighter.

"I wish I could stay."

"Tell me why you can't."

"You know why. My life is across the ocean."

"You can write from anywhere. I want you here with me. Let me show you the world. I've thought this through and I know it can work." He pulled me in closer. "Say you'll stay."

My brows furrowed. "You're serious, aren't you?"

"I'm proper serious." He sighed in my ear.

I inhaled his scent as we slow-dragged to the fast songs and the slow ones after that. We stopped when it was time for Taylor and Levi to cut their cake. Levi and Mash shared a congratulatory embrace, and got on as they did earlier in the week.

"This is from the both of us," he said, placing an envelope in Levi's hand.

Outside the banquet room doors, lavender and dried flowers hurled in the air at the wedded couple. We saw them off, and the bridal and groom party packed their gifts in Taylor's parent's suite, closing out our final orders.

Mash and I disappeared to our room, picking up where we left off. We lied in bed laughing at the tele, snuggled close exchanging moments of passionate kisses, and gazed at each other in silence saying how we felt with our eyes.

He wiped my tears when they fell. Avoided eye contact with me as I packed. And stepped out to smoke when I added items from his luggage into my own.

"I want to take whatever I can to hold onto you," I said.

He stared at the floor from the edge of the bed in the middle of the night. I crept behind him, contemplating his request to abandon my life across the ocean.

While kissing and squeezing his shoulders, I listened to him sigh, studying the brooding brows above his distant eyes in the mirror. I wanted to shout, "Of course I'll stay with you," but I was afraid. Afraid to be alone in London without my friends and family nearby as a safety net. Afraid he was who I had been searching for and I would mess it up. Afraid to take a chance at a life I had not planned.

I asked, "This is going to sound weird, but may I have the t-shirt you're wearing?"

He removed my arms from around him, folded it neatly, and placed it in my bag. He sat in the chair near the mini bar, and poured himself a shot.

"Leave me something of yours as well."

"Like what?"

"Whatever you want me to have."

I huffed. "Can we at least discuss how and when we're going to see each other again?"

"I'll send you my schedule. You pick which city you want to come to, and I'll fly you in."

"What about you coming to see me?"

He refused to look at me. "I'll come when you tell me to."

"Are we okay?"

"Yeah. I just hate this day has finally come."

He threw his head back and gulped the harsh brown. I minced to the bar and stood in front of him, stroking his hair while pressing his head against my stomach. He looked up at me and told me he missed me already, then kissed the back of my hand while rubbing on the back of my thighs. I could never get enough of his hands touching on my body.

My legs withered from his fingertips. It was time. He knew it. I knew it. We had become addicted to one another. Sexually. Wholeheartedly. And our bodies could no longer fight for our rhythms to collide.

He grazed my nipples with his teeth. Toying with them. Forcing the nerves between my slit to pulse. My breasts gave him a salute. Pointing at the tip with each nip.

I stood in front of him, holding on to his shoulders with a muddled mind, wondering what was this hold he had on me. I was plagued by not knowing how I was going to get along back home without him.

Seductive kisses melted against my skin. His approach was tender this time with delicate strokes brushing up and down my back. Elongated kisses traced across my neck. Then, he stood and danced with me in circles beside the bar.

The song between us ended and he carried me to the bed. His fingers drew lines from my feet, all the way up my legs as if he were making a mental image of them to keep. Then, he kissed the exterior of my orifice with a closed mouth. Not once. Not twice. Several slow and gentle pecks, observing the shocks in between.

I squirmed as I wanted him inside of me, but he made me wait for him. His tongue licked me everywhere it could reach, Frenching my lower lips as if it had a tongue of its own.

I groused with my hands running through his hair. Sighing for him to ease the pain of my departure. And then he hovered over me. Waiting to give me what I craved.

He lingered above my desperate begging body. He looked into my eyes and rubbed his thumbs across my cheeks. He traced the outline of my bitten lips with his index finger. Inducing a weakness in me from impeding attention.

"Put it in." I begged.

He refused, still studying me.

I pled again. "Mash, please let me feel you inside me."

He wouldn't give in to my demand. He was in control, showing me what I would miss if I left, though I missed him already.

I laid there patiently beneath him, gazing into his eyes. and brushing his face against mine. I could have gone mad from deprivation as I braced for his vast entrance.

"Unh," I whimpered, from gratification once the torture was over.

He grinned as if he was looking forward to hearing the

sound leave my lips. Back and forth we moved in unison, looking deep into each other's eyes.

"Stay," he whispered.

I looked away.

"Stay," he repeated, resting his head on my shoulder.

I gasped in between jabs, never responding to his request, and losing the battle of holding back my tears. My grind from below excited him, but my tears forced him to break our gaze.

He wrapped my legs around his waist, moaning insatiably from the build-up. My ass encompassed his pressing palms, bringing me up further as he drilled for my black gold.

"Let me hear you say my name one last time," he ordered.

"Maximus," I moaned.

"Again."

"It's not the last time," I said.

"Again."

"Maximus." I cried.

"I love you."

The climax was bittersweet. I hadn't felt so good and so bad at the same time ever in my life. I was riddled with guilt, and without explanation, but mainly perplexed at his word choice. *One Last Time.*

Distance doesn't work well for most relationships, and I took his words to mean he was giving up before we tried. I listened to him drift off, then slithered from underneath his arm. So much was on my mind that I couldn't sleep.

I texted Khai:

You up?

I am now.

Can I come down? Please?

Sure thing.

Khai sat propped up on the bed looking at me with her-*this better be good*-face. I sat at the foot and spilled my guts.

"You know how you've always been there for me?"

Her voice dragged. "Yeah."

"I don't know what I would do if I didn't have you in my life."

"If this is about Taylor and Isla being shady to you, don't sweat it. We're friends, but sometimes friends get jealous of one another. It'll blow over."

"Maybe. But you know how the two of them have their thing, and you and I have our thing, and all four of us have Shannon?"

"Yeah."

"Well, this is a me and you thing." I paused. "He asked me to stay, Khai."

"Stay as in move here?"

"I guess. I haven't asked him to go into detail about it. He just keeps repeating "stay, stay, stay.""

"Do you want to?"

"I have no fucking clue what I want! I wanted a good man. I found him. A gotdamn diamond in the rough to be exact. I've wanted someone to love me. And not just say it. But show it. And he does that. But why does he have to live on the other fuckin' side of the world? If I stay, I'm giving up my life—for a man…That's sounds so bizarre don't you think?"

"It is quite a pickle. Especially this day and age when we are all talking about women's rights, and the fight for equality."

"And here I am considering doing something as bonkers as staying in another country for a man."

Khai's brows raised. "But he's a good man. You said so yourself."

"Is he? We've known him for seven days. No, no, no I can't stay. My mother would kill me. I'd lose my best friend. I'd be

over here all alone. Just forget I even came down here and bothered you."

I stood to leave, then sat back down in confusion. Silence sat
between us as Khai stared at me with half a smile on her lips,
and half a laugh at the back of her throat.

"Nadia, did you come down here so I could tell you what
to do?"

"Maybe. No. I don't know. Probably."

"Well, I can't make this decision for you. But I will say, you
should clarify what he means by stay. Maybe he wants you to
stay for a few extra days. That wouldn't be so bad. Ask him."

I perked up. "A few days wouldn't be a problem."

"Exactly. But you have to have the conversation."

"And what if he means a few weeks?"

"Then, you need to decide if he's worth you giving him that
kind of time and attention. What are you afraid of?"

"That this will end like it did with Dylan. Being used and
betrayed and thrown away like a piece of trash. That if I stay,
he'll get bored with me and ship me home when he's ready, and
I will have lost all of my self-respect." I wiped away my tears
before they fell.

"This one is nothing like Dylan. I've seen how Vanilla Ice
looks at you. And you him." She giggled.

My mouth fell open, and my tears fell from the hard laugh
that echoed from my stomach. Trying to catch my breath I
uttered, "Don't make me laugh." But we both fell over
guffawing.

"Everyone saw how he looks at you. I bet you didn't notice
all eyes were on you two when you were dancing. And I saw
his face when he showed up tonight. He lit up when he found
you."

"He said he loves me."

"And I believe he does."

"I said it, too."

She jumped up from the bed and clapped her hands. "I knew it!"

I lowered my head. "You think I'm crazy, don't you?"

"I think you're scared more than anything. Look, if you stay, you won't lose me girl. Hell, your man is rich. He can fly me back and forth when you say the word."

I laughed.

"By the way. Before you go, I need to remind you that you owe me something."

"What?"

"The 411. Is it good, girl?"

"Do all donkeys have a cross on their back?" I sashayed away with a grin.

Khai screamed into her pillow.

❧ ✈

MASH WAS in the same spot I left him in. I crawled next to him and kissed his arm, his face, his shoulder, and his neck while watching him sleep. I put my foot under his shin and stared at the clock, waiting for the alarm to sound.

Eventually, the night got the best of me and I woke to a ringing telephone, and a fully dressed Mr. Sharper. He sat in the lounge as the housekeeping carts squeaked pushing past our room.

"They begin early, don't they," I said.

He glanced in my direction with half an impish grin.

I threw on the sweat suit I arrived in, and zipped up my final bag. Mash gathered our load. I trailed close behind him, and noticed that the click on the door triggered him.

He stopped short on the way to the elevator. He held my hand, then offered to drive me to the airport.

"That won't be necessary, but thank you for offering."

Our fingers entangled on the ride down until we reached the

lobby floor. Mash settled the bill while I stood with the other passengers waiting to board the shuttle. My hands began shaking as I stood on the curb, until I felt his cover mine. He wrapped me in his arms one final time. I quivered from his touch.

"You okay?" he asked.

I nodded yes, lying as best I could.

"Stay with me," he said.

The girls handed their luggage to the attendant, then approached us.

Khai extended her hand. "It was nice meeting you, Mash."

"Nice meeting you, too. All of you. Hopefully we'll get to hang out again soon."

I trembled.

"And thank you for taking us on the bar crawl. When you come to the States, we'll treat you right." Shannon shook his hand.

Mash nodded. "I'm going to hold you to that."

Khai looked me up and down, and then in the eyes. She placed her arms around me, and I dropped a tear, visibly shaking in front of everyone.

She squeezed my shoulders, then said to Mash. "You take care of our girl now."

Shannon turned around and questioned me with her eyes.

"Take care of our girl?" she mouthed.

I widened my eyes and handed my keys to Khai. "I'll call you if I need you. Love you and be safe."

Shannon's mouth dropped to her feet. She put her arms around Khai and I, and we hugged like teens going off to college.

The driver split us up, calling for the last round of passengers. I watched them board the shuttle, shaking in my boots, second guessing my decision as the bus pulled out of the lot.

Mash swung me around like a merry go round. He plastered his sweet lips on mine with an audience watching.

"Are you ready to take me home?"

He gloated. "You have no idea."

Shannon and Khai tapped on the tinted glass making heart symbols with their fingers.

"Love you!" They shouted from the shuttle as the engine throttled, and I was carried away.

I shouted it back as Mash loaded my bags in the car. "To the outskirts we go," I said, living on a prayer and taking a chance with my heart.

The part of me that was closed off for many years reopened and began writing a new chapter.

OUI

Stay. A few extra days, a week, a month? I needed clarification, but delayed asking Mash for an end date on our arrangement. I feared that conversation would ruin the perfect vibe we had going. Finishing each other's sentences. Moving in sync. Our chemistry felt like a natural bond. Him being the H_2 to my O's.

He made me feel welcome in his house, persisting that I call it home. If he saw me working, he'd give me space. When he had a long day, I made sure he had room to breathe when he came home. I had access to money and his cars within a few days of my stay. And by the end of my first week as a guest of Maximus Sharper, I could no longer hold my tongue.

I set up the folding table and chairs in the middle of the kitchen, and cooked a simple meal—brown sugar salmon with butter whipped potatoes and Caesar salad. Fresh flowers spruced up the scene, and old R&B set the mood.

Mash came home and kissed my cheek as he always does when he greets me. His hand finds the same spot between my waist and my back, and no matter what kind of day he had, he let me know he was happy to see me with a smile.

"Dinner's ready. Follow me to the kitchen."

I listened to him tell me about his meetings, upcoming shows, and pit of the day.

"As always, seeing you is the peach," he said.

Once he unloaded his day to me, I casually threw in a curveball.

"The price of flights went up today. I need to book something weeks in advance for a good rate."

"The rate doesn't matter. I'll cover it. What date are you looking to fly?" He adjusted his frames.

The secret weapon in his arsenal turned out to be his Clark Kent personna. The Tom Welling version. The first time he came home wearing them after a day of meetings, I had to pull my sweater closed to hide my budding nipples. I loved when he wore those glasses. They gave him an extra check on the sexy scale as if he needed anything more to make me swoon him.

My mouth opened to speak, but my words took their time leaving as every move he made thereafter was in slow motion. "I was hoping we could discuss that. When do *you* want me to leave?"

He finished chewing. "Why would I want that?"

I licked my lips. "When you asked me to stay, what did you mean? A few days? A week?"

"Honestly, when I asked..." He set down his fork. "I didn't have an end date in mind."

"I don't wanna outstay my welcome is all."

He hypnotized me with his gaze. "You still don't get it, do you?"

"I think I'm starting to. But I don't wanna be wrong."

We lunged across the flimsy table. It surprisingly held up against us fucking in the middle of the meal. This had become my new normal. A simple look, or accidental graze against my skin, led to my legs being lifted over my head, or me bent over the couch, burning from the passionate fire between us.

I had no idea when I was going home. The time had come for me to face my mother who'd sent message after message to that question.

By the end of week two, I was with him in Paris. I followed my lover to the city of lights, running down narrow streets, eating delectable pastries, visiting historic museums, and gaining access to hidden gems only people like him knew about.

His access to places was notable, and during this trip I learned how important he was. I was blinded by his kindness and attention in the beginning, overlooking how the world viewed him and his work. Quickly, I became acclimated to the world of fame.

I took photographs of old dated buildings, and snaps of fashionable people coming and going. I picked up on certain words I remembered from French class in high school, and used a few of them when conversing with the hotel staff. Those interactions guided me to the best pastry shop in Paris while Mash was busy with sound check.

I sat on the balcony of our penthouse suite, over indulging on chocolate croissants and observing the people of the city. The Eiffel Tower glittered in the backdrop, and the streets buzzed below. The owner of a café across the street, swept the sidewalk just before turning her signage to *fermee*.

Moments later she locked its doors, and set off holding the hand of a little girl whom I assumed was her daughter. I watched them until they turned the corner. They reminded me of me and my mother. How she'd hold my hand tight whenever we went out in public.

I dialed her number.

"Your grandmother and I had a nice chat about you, little girl," she answered.

"Good things I hope. How is she? How are you?"

"I'm my usual self, but your grandmother is not. She said you haven't called her in weeks. You normally call her every day."

"She's right. I haven't been myself lately."

"Oh, we know." My mother scoffed.

"Is she mad? Are you?"

"Truthfully, as long as you're safe, we're fine with whatever it is you're doing. What exactly *are you* doing? Besides laying up with a strange man. And spare me the details."

"I'm writing. And traveling." I gripped on the phone a little tighter. "I'm in Paris right now. It's beautiful, Ma. We should have done things like this. Ya know?"

"Traveling wasn't our thing. I'm glad you're doing it though. Is your friend with you right now?"

"Not at the moment."

"Well tell him as long as he doesn't hurt you, he won't have anything to worry about. Your friends have given me his address, so I know how to find him."

"I'm in good hands, Ma."

"Seems so."

"I just wanted to tell you that, and tell you I miss you, and I'll see you soon. I love you."

"I love you, too, baby."

Weight lifted from my shoulders. I thought calling my mother was going to be the hardest phone call of my life. I expected to be chewed out for my reckless behavior and rash decisions. But receiving her support helped me feel better about the chance I took to stay.

Afterwards, I called my favorite person in the world, Grams. And when she didn't cut me with her sharp tongue, I exhaled on a full stomach of chocolate and dough, and relaxed as the wind swept up high where I sat. I embraced the happiness I'd been feeling for the past few weeks. No longer waiting for the shoe to drop. Finally embracing the decision I made as the correct one.

A CAR WAS SENT for me hours later. Before the concert, I stopped at the postal stand in the lobby and mailed myself a postcard with the words, *'You came. You saw. You found it.'*

Nightlife in the city reminded me of the years I spent in college. Seeing the crowds of women laugh and having a good time together, made me wish my friends were sharing this experience with me.

I smiled at the group and wondered, *'Is that how they looked when they came here?'*

Flashes of made up images came into my mind of them walking in packs and shopping and gossiping. But then I thought about my trip to Spain and daydreamed of the blue water, the emotional high I felt on the beach, and the caress of Mash keeping me warm in the night. *'They would have said fuck Paris too if they were me,'* I thought, then snapped out of it.

The women were no longer in my view. I sent Khai a picture I took of myself with the Eiffel Tower in the background. She replied with a picture of bowling shoes, and I laughed out loud in the car. I missed them, but wasn't missing out on anything back home except shit talking in a smoke-filled alley stinking up my hair.

I arrived at the venue. A stagehand escorted me to Mash's dressing room. Backstage was reminiscent of Taylor's wedding day: stressful, fast-paced, lively, and crowded.

The room was tucked away in a dark corner of the building. It needed a major facelift, cleaning, and paint job. It might have been easier to demolish what looked like an abandoned pit stop where hobos slept.

I was afraid to sit or touch anything, so I stood on alert and roamed the space, realizing it looked the way it did because it was indeed a pit stop of historic figures. Acts from all over the world had signed the walls, the mirrors, the dressers, and the chairs. It was a filthy rite of passage for entertainers.

I searched for Mash's name until the stage hand returned for me.

"He's ready for you," he said, taking me stage-right with the other VIPs.

This gig was nothing like the one under the tent in Glastonbury. The crowd was massive and electrifying, clamored together in solidarity cheering on each artist. Somehow, a few worked their way backstage to meet the acts when the show was over. It was unsettling to watch woman after woman throw themselves at the artists. Including the one I considered was mine.

I stood far away in a dimly lit shadow of a boulder. Watching. Taking it all in. The action. The mystery. The thrill. The flirting.

Mash was humble and acknowledged all those who approached him. It was a great look for him. I, on the other hand, had been given a front row seat to a world my insecurities could not handle. I was jealous, and that brought back a world of deceit I had no desire to relive.

The stage hand found me in the corner. He escorted me down a hallway to a tunnel where the artists come and go. I sat in the car for nearly thirty minutes. Stewing, while I waited for Mash to come out.

He looked beat when he finally exited the building.

"All done," I asked.

"That was insane at the end. Where were you?"

"I got lost in the crowd, so I stepped back to give the fans their space."

"Did you enjoy the show?"

"I was blown away. I must admit. I didn't know you were this big of a deal. Seeing it firsthand is different from reading tabloids."

"Stop." He covered his face and blushed.

I could have and should have let it end there, but doing what I normally do, I continued to reach.

"How do you handle all of those fans coming at you like that?"

"What are you getting at?"

I scoffed. "I'm not too keen on seeing women put their hands all over you."

"Imagine being the person who doesn't like people putting their hands all over you. It sucks, but it comes with the territory of what I do."

"I didn't think of it that way." I bit my lip.

"You're about to see more of it. I just got an updated schedule, and we'll be hitting the road pretty hard over the next few weeks, so get ready."

We were in the land of the oui, but he said we—making plans for us without my input or say. And I rolled with it.

PASSPORT

For days I was alone as preparation for the upcoming events required Mash to be at rehearsals, studios sessions, and meetings. I kept busy enrolling in exercise and dance classes, and people watching at cafes where I wrote submission pieces about travel, western news from an eastern perspective, and romance short stories for online mags and pay per episode apps.

A week and a half later, I was in Cannes for a film festival, the first stop on the excursion where Mash was hired to appear at a few parties. He surprised me with passes to screenwriting workshops and movie premieres with A-list celebs to keep me occupied. I fell in love with him more for acknowledging my interests, and not seeing me as a companion to follow him around all day.

Between the workshops and seminars and premieres, I roamed the streets to sight-see and taste-test. One day the sun shone so bright, I basked in the sun of the French Riviera until it was time to link up. Mash and I gambled in a casino for a few hours before sailing on a private yacht with one of his industry associates.

The snooty and elite lounged on the vessel. Models walked around in skimpy bathing suits, champagne was served whenever you turned around, A-list actors and actresses acting holier than thou, and musicians crossing over into film snorted lines out in the open.

"Don't stare," Mash whispered.

"How can I not? I ain't never been to no shit like this."

The look on his face was priceless. His hand slipped around my waist and he pulled me close.

"Never?"

"Never. Mary Jane. Sure. But powder. Un uh."

"I swear you're so cute. We don't have to stay long."

Every time a famous woman tugged on Mash's arm, or one of the half naked models tapped him on the shoulder or smiled in his face, my insecurity went into overdrive. I'd never been in the position to compare myself to famous or powerful women. I felt inferior to them. Constantly wondered how I measured up, or could compete with women like them who were desired and made lots of money. I didn't like it being a penniless shadow.

I was happy when the boat docked near our resort. We took a night stroll through the villas, pussyfooting around what happened on the boat.

"You were different back there. Talk to me."

"Was I?"

He stopped walking.

I pulled him along. "Just wasn't my crowd."

"Is that all?"

"Yep."

He knew I was lying. He could feel the shift, but didn't pressure me to say. We continued our walk in silence as I reminded myself that a lack of confidence is a turnoff. I said it to myself over and over until that timid feeling passed.

I wrapped my fingers around his. "I'm fine," I said.

"You sure?"

I assured him with a kiss, knowing eventually I would be.

THE NEXT MORNING we flew to Amsterdam. Two days in the city didn't give us time to explore the way I had hoped. Amid the rumors of it being well known for its red-light district, I wasn't interested in seeing sex-trafficked women work. I preferred to visit the museums, and taste the world-famous crepes as research for a travel submission, but time didn't allow it. Neither did the congestion of the city. I bust my ass riding a bike as the streets were overly crowded, and spent the rest of our short stint there in the hotel room with my feet up.

When it was time to return to London, I was still a little sore from the fall. It felt good to lounge around in a familiar place and fully heal.

The down time made me homesick. Mash was busy with work. I had the house to myself most of the day, and rejections from my submissions humbled me.

I checked the price of flights as I'd done before. Feeling tired and lonely with nothing but time on my hands, I felt like I was losing myself in someone else's world. His world.

As exciting as it was, it wasn't my world. I wasn't living my life. I was busy being rejected and clueless how I would keep everything afloat back home without money coming in.

I had access to Mash's money, but never being in a situation-ship like ours before, I didn't know how to say, "Hey, cut me a check to cover my bills back home." I figured that was the easiest way to get a pink slip. So, without discussing it with Mash, I booked a flight into CLT for the same night he was due in Barcelona.

I had three days to tell him, but couldn't muster the courage. There never was a good time to bring it up when he came home.

He was always spent from preparations, and telling me everyday how good it was to see me.

Every night he greeted me with a kiss, showered, ate, and laid under me while I keyed my soul away—in need of something to be published to prove I was worthy of my craft.

With nothing to lose, I submitted a synopsis of my Mandarin piece to a production company in search of fresh, own voices. The next morning, I lightly stroked Mash's shoulder.

"Maximus," I whispered.

He twisted and grunted. Mumbling something inaudible with his eyes closed.

"I have to tell you something."

"It must be bad news," he muttered.

"I booked a flight home."

His eyes opened wide. He lifted up and sat back against the headboard and refused to look at me.

"I felt this coming in Cannes. Are you sick of me? What is it? The late nights? The shows?"

"I'm not sick of you. I just need to go home for a little while. I was thinking maybe you could come see me when your schedule opens up."

"What's waiting for you there…back home?"

"My life is waiting there. My mother. My friends. I need to check on my house. Visit my Grams. Submit to publications that will actually publish my work and earn a paycheck."

"So, it's money? I gave you access to the account, which you haven't used by the way." He sighed. "Why are you really rushing to go back home?"

"I'm homesick! And I feel like I'm not doing anything except be your shadow puppet. I'm not used to being a kept woman. I'm used to having my own. Calling things my own. What's so wrong with wanting to see my people? I've been here so long I'm practically a citizen."

He finally looked at me, but it felt like he was looking

through me and I couldn't take it. I left the bed and threw on my robe.

"Are you done?"

"I haven't had one article published since I've been here? I feel like I'm losing myself."

"I didn't know. You never said."

"You never asked." I exhale deeply. "I ask myself what would have happened if I didn't stay."

"I would have taken time off to visit you. But you stayed, and I thought if I played my cards right you would never want to leave. It never occurred to me that you would get tired of being here."

"I love being here with you. I'm just…"

I sauntered near the window and looked into the darkness, searching for the words to end my sentence. He followed me and placed his chin on my shoulder. His hands wrapped around my waist.

"Do I make you happy?"

"Very much so," I said, leaning my head against his.

"I don't like this scowl on your pretty face. What can I do to fix this?"

"Maybe take some time off and come home with me."

"Consider it done. I give you my word. We'll set a date and make it happen." He stroked my cheek. "I'll have my agency move some things around and we'll go. Okay?"

"Thank you."

"I planned something special for us this weekend. Say you're still coming with me."

"Have I ever let you down?"

"Not once." He turned my face towards him and kissed my lips. "So, this is what it's like to argue with you?"

My face burned with embarrassment. "That was not an argument. More like a disagreement."

"I don't know…you got a little feisty a second ago."

"You call that feisty?"

He grinned. "It kind of turned me on. Do you need help getting the rest of it out of you?"

"Oh no." I slipped from his embrace. "I have work to do."

"So do I." He picked me up and carried me to the bed.

"I can't say no to you and that worries me."

I was curious about these special plans Mash mentioned. In the morning, I cancelled my flight home and packed for Barcelona.

Once again, my feet touched the soil of Spain. Its colored beauty could not be ignored from the sky, but to see the murals and buildings up close were breathtaking.

Familiar with the city, Mash took me to see the popular ins and outs and galleries. He served as my tour guide for two days, on guard for pickpockets, and keeping me close.

We followed a map of the well-known historic cathedrals. My favorite part was our stroll in the Gothic Quarter. The narrow lanes and eerie architecture inspired me to try my hand at writing darker material.

"I'm inspired here," I said to him.

"Are you glad you didn't leave?"

"I am," I said, spotting a shopping market up ahead.

Kiosks with novelty and keepsake items targeted for tourists filled the lot. My eyes locked in on a booth selling wire-beaded handmade rings. The intertwining of a black and blue band spoke to me, and with permission the attendant allowed me to slip it on my finger.

"Fits perfect. Made for you," he said.

Mash pulled out some Euros and it was mine.

"Make one to match for me?" He asked the owner. "How much?"

The artist took his measurements. "Come back in thirty."

With a half-hour to kill, we ate street food, sat and listened to a band performing near the water, then returned to the stand.

The craftsman earned a healthy tip when he presented us with matching bracelets, identical to the pattern of the rings. I couldn't stop admiring my matching set in the sun. It reminded me of the hand-crafted jewelry sold downtown on the market in Charleston.

I stuck my hand out and dangled my wrist side to side at least a dozen times, fascinated at how the colors moved and shined in the sunlight.

"You love it that much?" Mash teased.

"I do. I respect the work of creative people. And I love to support artists. I know it's only wire and beads, but working with beads requires talent."

"You can have my bracelet. One for each arm."

I snatched it quickly. "Thank you. No backsies."

He snatched it back. "One more thing." He slipped the bracelet on my wrist. "Marry me tomorrow."

"Be serious."

"I am. It's the only reason I wanted this ring made."

"I thought you just wanted to match mine."

"Yes. As husband and wife."

"My feisty side didn't scare you away?"

"I've had this on my mind for weeks now. That little fight wouldn't have changed my mind."

"You really wanna marry me? Tomorrow?"

"I had this whole thing planned out for when we went home, but I don't want to wait. Let's do it here. Yeah?"

He gazed at me with love in his eyes. I couldn't break away from the hold they had on me.

"Tell me the worst thing about you," I said.

"I'm jealous."

"So am I."

"I've seen enough to know I will weather any storm with you. Say you'll be my wife. Say you'll marry me."

The concierge in our hotel located a priest to perform the

ceremony on the beach. I bought an inexpensive white sundress in the village, and tied white flowers around thread in the hotel room sewing kit. I pinned the headdress to my hair and walked barefoot on the beach with a bouquet of calla lilies in my hand as the wind pushed me toward my groom.

My soulmate waited for me in his white t-shirt and slacks he bought from a general store. He proved that even in cheap clothes, he still had that it factor.

The wind and the mist blew my straight hair curly, while the sun blessed us with light. Strangers stopped and watched us elope. No big show and no drama. Just the two of us, holding hands on a beautiful day vowing to love each other forever. Becoming one.

MRS

Our bond was consummated several times over. Flickering candles and calla lilies spread on the floor. The tenderness of his touch because we were official. The wind against my breast the second time we made love on the balcony when he unleashed the beast I had come to know. The sound of my back tapping against the glass door from our insatiable habit.

Nothing could have removed the smile I carried for days. My husband couldn't have picked a better moment or place to ask for my hand. Life seemed surreal with him as mine. But he was. Mine all mine.

As we traveled across Europe, I looked down at the greens of the land and the stillness of the ocean. I crossed those terrains with and because of him. I had to pinch myself at times thinking I would wake up from a dream. But this was my life. My only worry from that point on was to not mess it up.

Instead of searching for flights back to America, I was scheduling when and where we would honeymoon, researching dual citizenship, and cooking up how to share my news with my mother and my friends.

In the meantime, I kept busy regarding my residency. The response from the embassy took days, and the information we needed turned out to be overly complicated. I had to prove I was living with Maximus for over a week, then we could apply for a license in 21 days to make our union legal in the U.K.. I also had to apply for a visa. The only visa I was ever interested in was the kind that swipes.

During the wait period to finalize my status, four days opened up on Mash's tight schedule.

"I picked where we should go on our honeymoon," I said.

"Where are we going?"

"Italy."

It was the only place I could get the perfect wedding gift—the best pizza in the world, and I'd get to meet my mother-in-law.

Valeria Pasini Sharper was stunning. Frail and tanned with strong cheekbones and wavy chestnut brown hair. Mash looked a lot like her. She cried at the sight of him standing in her doorway, speaking her language with what I assumed ended with many emphases after each word.

"Vita! Vita!" she shouted.

Thumping noises came from the top of the house. A cute, middle-aged woman peeped around the wall and shouted more words in Italian. I stood patiently by the door, watching the two women pinch Mash's cheeks and chin.

There was an abundance of hugs and kisses and prayer hands and love for him. It was the first time I saw him cry. And that made me shed a few tears by proxy.

Shortly, they settled down and he reached for my hand. I stepped by his side and he introduced me as his wife. Valeria held her face then held mine.

"Bambino," she said.

My eyes widened and I waved my hands. "No bambino. No bambino."

I was offended, but kept quiet. Vita then stood next to her and eyed me from head to toe. My heart pounded literally being in Valeria's hands.

She and Vita held a brief conversation in their language. I looked over to Mash for help. He placed his arm around me and joined the discussion.

Valeria sweetly said, *"Figlia."*

She and Vita hugged me, gave me an extra once over, then pulled me by my arms to the sofa. I didn't understand a word the three of them were saying, but I picked up on *telefono* when Vita started making phone calls.

Within the hour, the house was packed with cousins and uncles from all over Vomero. The news Maximus was home travelled quickly, and the news he married a cocoa-colored American surprisingly went better than I expected.

His family showed me love and made me feel welcome, speaking in very little English and forcing me to eat. Our union received the warmest reception as his family blasted music and cooked food way into the night.

The former Mrs. Sharper wouldn't allow us to stay in the hotel we reserved. She forced us to stay with her in Mash's old room with the thin walls, full-size bed, and loose headboard. We laughed most of the night, trying to sneak in a quick one, eventually giving up and dozing off.

By morning the house was already filled with family. Some who spent the night because it was a special occasion, and others who wanted to get a jump on the festivities. It was a repeat of the previous day. Family all around. Music blasting. People dancing. Matriarchs cooking. Children running amuck. And everyone singing.

Before the sun set in the evening, my new cousins drove us around the never-ending hills to a spot overlooking the city and Mount Vesuvius in the distance. The buildings looked like they were stacked on top of one another, but the sight was one to behold.

Cousin Primo convinced us to check out a sports bar where he bragged to any and every one that his cousin was famous. I put on a brave face as I watched everyone, except me go berserk when a team scored a point in the soccer match on the television. The place rocked with stomps and cheers. Celebration chimes dinged from every corner, and beer splashed from tall glasses toasting around the hall.

The family kept the same energy when we returned to the house with more food, music still blasting, and more blankets laid out for the night. Seeing Mash around his family was an image I would always remember. He came from beautiful, loving people who instilled their values in him somehow from a distance. It was a side of him I needed to see, to cancel any doubt he was the one for me.

In the middle of the night he woke me, nibbling on my face. "You picked the best place for our honeymoon. What made you decide to come here?"

"Ibiza would have been ideal, but I know we're going back there this summer. And I wanted to meet your mom. Plus, I didn't want to go anywhere tropical."

"Why not?"

"Because I've been too embarrassed to tell you, I fall into the stereotype when it comes to water," I mumbled beneath my pillow.

"But we're near the coast and sea."

"I know, but you don't think of boats, and oceans when you think of Pompeii. You think of the volcano and landmarks."

"True." He scowled. "But what stereotype?"

"I can't swim. I've tried to learn, but I can't hold my breath long underwater. And when I try to move in the water, I go nowhere. It's quite comical."

"I can teach you."

"No one can teach me. My parents wasted money on lessons for several summers. I will only frustrate you."

"No, you won't. It'll be the first thing I teach you. The second will be how to make a proper mix."

"My mixes are just fine."

He tapped my nose. "Remember I've seen your playlists."

I squeezed his in return. We wrestled and giggled until I caved under pressure to give him a chance.

I warned him. "I'll give it one lesson. But I'm telling you I'm pretty bad."

"I love a challenge. I'll have you swimming like a fish by the end of the summer."

"God, you're confident. Go back to sleep."

"Sleep's not on my mind." He placed my hand on his erection.

"The walls are too thin," I whispered. "You know someone will hear us."

I rubbed his cock regardless of my excuse. He was free in my hands growing harder by the second. He slipped his finger inside of me and gnawed on my neck. The bed squeaked when he got too excited and lifted my legs so he could taste my lips.

"I don't care if they hear us. I want you now," he said.

I sighed. "I hate saying no to you."

"Then don't."

I slipped under the covers and kissed him softly on the tip of his head, then slicked him with strong pulls from my throat to my lips. My plan was to suck him off quietly, so the family wouldn't hear the headboard knock against the wall, or squeak from the bed as I was being pillaged. But Mash struggled being quiet from my stellar performance.

I rose from below and stared at him. "They are going to talk about me if you don't keep it down." I placed my finger over his lips and treated him to a few more licks.

When it became too much for him, he motioned against the

bed. It squeaked to a rhythm and I gave up. Mash hopped to his feet and pulled me up. I dropped to my knees to finish the job, gliding my hands against his abs, and looking directly in his eyes. He was no different from most men that can't take that type of power from a woman when they're in that position.

The taste of salt tinged my tongue. I froze and grinned at him, knowing he was putty in my hands. He stopped me short of my victory, lifted me from the floor, and bent me over facing the wall.

A gleeful sigh escaped my mouth when our skin slapped in rhythm. Mash grunted working me from the back. I was sure he woke the house.

The painful pleasure overpowered me, but held in my moans. Silence, not by his hands, would not be tolerated by my husband. He lifted me higher and pressed my face on the wall, kissing my profile as one hand wrapped around my neck.

He closed the gap between us. A light choke held me in place. The asphyxiated sounds of me gasping put him over the edge, and he came violently inside of me with a boisterous finish. It was as if being on vacation made him not have a care in the world. He was unconcerned about the listening ears, whereas I restrained myself vocally with a fist in my mouth.

The next morning, I was greeted with snickers from the aunts and my mother-in-law in the kitchen.

"What a beautiful glow you have this morning," said one of them in English.

The rest of them chuckled at my expense.

"It must be the water here," I replied. "Buongiorno."

"Mm hmm." Valeria smiled. "Buongiorno."

Italian words circled the room with giggles between them—*bambino* and *presto* frequently in their exchange. I smiled to let them know I knew that they were going in on me.

Mash rescued me for a day out. Just the two of us. Traffic was heavy on the short drive to Pompeii, but the scenic route made it worthwhile during the stall. Picturesque buildings and famous, mythological mosaics livened up the route.

The closer we were to the city, we withdrew from our original plans of visiting the ruins, and roamed the streets instead. The highlight of the day was finally tasting what I heard was the best pizza in the world. I wasn't lied to. It was *magnifico*.

I moaned with every bite, and didn't speak until I met the owner. After explaining how far I traveled to taste his heavenly pie, and commending him on its supreme flavor, he whispered his secret in my ear.

"*L'acqua naturale.*"

Before returning to a house full of family, we strolled down the cobblestoned streets in the neighborhood, enjoying the starry night sky, searching for zodiac signs and visible planets. We picked up cartons of gelato for the little ones, and spent our final night with family trading stories—Mash translated for me, until I called it a night with a belly so full it nearly burst.

The night ended with a surprise from Valeria. In front of the entire family, she placed a ring in Mash's hand. He translated her wish which was for him to place her mother's ring on my finger, and made me promise to continue the tradition.

I repeated, "*Lo prometto,*" and the family cheered as Mash slid the heirloom on my hand.

The house remained filled with Pasini's for a final night, but it didn't stop us from repeating last night's activities—most likely being cheered on from every room in the house.

The next morning, we returned to business as usual. I wasn't eager to go with Maximus to Copenhagen. I even suggested that I depart for London and that he go without me.

"It's only for a night. I can be home settling in for our life together."

"There's no way I'm sending you back to our house without me. I have to carry you over the threshold, Mrs. Sharper." He lifted my chin. "Everything will be fine."

The concert in Copenhagen headlined Harv Legend. The name put a bitter taste in my mouth. I laid low the moment we checked into the hotel. I was beat from all of the travel and hadn't a real moment to breathe and process it all. Lounging in the hotel room for one night was an all around genius plan to avoid conflict and recharge.

I missed out on the famous crepe station, museums, and local faves Mash raved about. I didn't bother to unpack. I was ready to depart as soon as the lights went out in the arena, but I was asleep when he arrived in the room sometime overnight. Just as spent as I was, he laid next to me fully clothed, and we slept in until the morning.

We worked together to catch our flight during checkout. He stood in line at the bistro to fetch us coffee and scones. I stood in line to settle the bill at the front desk.

"Thank you for staying with us." The clerk handed me the receipt.

I reached for it, and a hand snatched it away from my grasp.

"So, we meet again. I thought you were long gone back to America." Harv Legend grinned on the side of his mouth, continuing to be persistently annoying.

"Hello, again. I hear you had an amazing show last night. Congrats. Now if you'll excuse me." I reached for the printout.

He switched it to his other hand. "How do you know we had a good show?"

"My husband told me."

"Husband? You and Mash?"

"Yes. Now if you'll please give me that so I can be on my way."

He folded the receipt in half. "Queens belong with Kings, yeah." He extended the paper toward me, then grabbed my hand.

I jerked away. "Don't do that."

Toying with me, he presented the slip and took it away. I huffed in frustration.

"Mash is a proper bloke, but he's not for you, Queen. He don't know what to do with a Queen like you."

I held my hand out the print.

He studied me, then finally placed it in my hand. "And here I thought I got lucky running into you. Remember my words. Queens belong with Kings." His hand brushed my shoulder.

I maneuvered backwards. Cat got my tongue as Mash appeared behind him. He reached forward and slapped Harv's hand from my shoulder, then stood in front of me.

"I thought we already went through this, mate."

Harv stood there in shock with a dumb look on his face. "I hear congratulations are in order. Seems like you would have mentioned that last night. But then again." He scoffed. "We know why you didn't. You two be easy."

"What's he talking about?" I asked.

"Harv, don't disrespect my wife again."

"Calm down big *mon. You no wan it wit a real bad mon.*"

"Grimey fuck!" Mash groaned.

"Can we get out of here?" I asked.

Harv turned around. "Oh you're a tough guy now?"

Mash balled his fists. "I think you want to see if I'm a tough guy."

I pulled on his arm. "I'm ready to leave. People are staring at us. Please."

I walked off. He followed me to the transport. As he caught up with me, he held my hand.

"You okay?"

"I'm fine."

And we left it at that until our eyes locked on the plane.

"Thank you for standing up for me," I said.

He kissed my forehead.

"I'm sorry that happened. I tried to handle it."

His eyes turned serious. "Don't apologize for him. He was being a total wanker."

"Ya know you said you were jealous, but you also have a bit of a temper. Promise me, you won't get into any trouble."

"You don't have to worry about me."

But I was worried. Not because I was naïve, or believed life was a fairytale even though mine had been lately. I was worried if I had gotten out of my way, and into his.

ALERT AFTER ALERT buzzed his phone when we landed. Mash's demeanor changed after reading the first message from his manager, Davie. His eyes tightened as the messages poured in. That temper I spoke of just hours ago was rearing its ugly head right in front of me.

I said nothing as he quietly fumed, staring at the vein swelling in his neck. I asked myself again, *'How could I not be worried?'*

Something was going on. He didn't care to share. The ride home was so quiet I heard the tires rolling on the road. The grimace on his face lasted until we made it home.

"Ready?" He asked.

I was stunned that he spoke. "For what?"

He lifted me in his arms and carried me inside. "Welcome home, Mrs. Sharper."

"I can get used to you calling me that." I kissed him. "And I can tell something is bothering you. Let me know if there's something I can do to help."

"You being here is enough." He put me down. "I need to make some calls. You get yourself relaxed and allow me to make up this morning to you."

Mash lit a joint out by the pool to handle his business. I unpacked our bags, put in a load of laundry, shampooed my hair and set the mood in our bedroom while the conditioner set. I cooked like a madwoman to help us wind down. I turned the rotting bananas into a banana nut loaf, and crushed fresh tomatoes and spices into a heavenly chili that floated through the house.

Mash had been on his phone since we returned. I checked on him a few times while he was out back. Whatever he was dealing with looked intense. But the more he blew on his smokes he mellowed out—or so I thought.

He called for me from the living room. "Put on your bathing suit!"

I ignored him.

"Let's go!" He called for me a second time.

"I just washed my hair!" I yelled back.

He came inside and cornered me in the kitchen. He was high as a kite. His bloodshot eyes and goofy smirk concerned me.

"Outside. Now." He demanded.

I threw on my suit and grabbed towels for the both of us. When I slid the door open I overheard him on a call.

A gentleman repeated, "We've got to fix this! We've got to fix this!"

"She's my wife. Cancel all future shows with him."

My worst fear had come true. My being in his life was creating chaos. I gripped the door handle, frozen in time, listening to the conversation while my mind got the best of me.

"I'm sure if he knew she was your wife he would have never disrespected you," said the male voice on the phone.

"On the contrary, he knew she was with me."

"Mash, what were you thinking getting married? It goes against the image we've worked so hard to give you. Your brand is at risk if word gets out you have a wife. Girls see you as the hot deejay they want to spend a night with, and the shows sell based on that fantasy. Women are 70% of your audience and fan base."

"Wow, Davie. And here I was thinking it was my mixes and musical talent drawing in the crowds."

"You and I both know this business is about more than talent. And you are talented kid, but this is the world we live in. You've got to work with me here. Do me a favor and keep the news of your nuptials quiet for now. I'll be in touch in a few days with word on how we're going to spin this."

The door jolted. I was busted eavesdropping.

"I heard every word. I'm sorry you're going through all of this because of me. I haven't told anyone we eloped yet, so the secret is safe with me."

"You're not a secret," he said.

"That's good to know." I exhaled sharply. "You know what, let's do this another day. I'm not in the mood to learn tonight."

"No. We're doing it now."

"Are you asking me, or telling me?"

He lifted me in his arms and jumped into the pool. We landed in the shallow side, and I stood in the water. I looked at him like he was crazy and wrestled to push away from him.

"Don't ever do that again!"

"Do what? Hold onto you?" He let me go, then his tone sweetened. "Show me what you can do."

"No. I don't want to."

He wrapped his arms around me. "I'm sorry."

Our bodies began to sway. He led and I followed. We danced to the music in our heads until he began to hum one. I laid my head on his shoulder while the anger he housed faded. Slowly, I let go of it too, and forgave him for throwing me in the water.

I went under and did the moves as I always had, then returned to the surface. Just as I told him, I was stagnant, but he didn't make fun of me.

"You're going to do just fine. Lesson one, go under again and open your eyes this time."

"No. It stings. I need goggles."

"Get comfortable not having them. Take your time. We've got all night."

I dunked my head under countless times, but never opened my eyes. I waited for him to grow impatient with me, but he frustrated me more with encouraging words to keep trying until I was no longer afraid.

Again and again I buried my head, insisting we give up, but he wouldn't allow it. My frustration with him soon turned into anger, and that anger finally paid off where I did it to get him off my ass.

We stared at each other for a brief moment beneath the surface. Mash smiled at me, then I rose to the top. I wiped my eyes and pushed my hair off my face.

My patient instructor swam to me and gave me a kiss. "Told you you could do it. That ends the first lesson."

The following afternoon we were back at it. He told me to get comfortable with opening my eyes in the water before learning how to hold my breath when below. Up and down he moved my head with a three count, relentless with his method. One hour—every day—I belonged to him in the water.

Kicks, strokes, and breathing techniques were my next challenge. By the end of the week I was floating on my back and swimming a small distance. It was a small victory for him. A huge one for myself. And it brought us closer than we had been before.

"I have to fulfill the contract I signed this weekend. It's the last one I'll have with Harv."

"Can I sit this one out?"

"You sure?"

I nodded.

"I'll return as soon as I can. Promise me you won't go in the pool without me. You've got it, but I haven't given you your certificate yet. Yeah."

"I swear to God if you present me with some ridiculousness in a frame, I'm cutting you off for a month."

He pinched my waist. "No, you won't."

Together we laughed because he was right.

It wasn't until later in the night and I had the house to myself that the intrusive thoughts crept in. I tried working, meal prepping, baking, and cleaning, but every moment that I sat still, there they were.

His career and brand was facing ruin because he was with me. He was now at odds with a longtime colleague because of me. He and his management were in a dispute because of me.

On top of that, I had to love him in secret and that hurt. A lot. My compromise to abandon my life seemed trivial compared to what he was facing. And being the common denominator in all of the madness didn't feel right. Didn't feel good either.

I opened a bottle of wine to put me down for the night. Mash called when I was on my third glass.

"How are you getting on without me?" he asked.

I chuckled. "Let's just say the house would give the Evans family a run for their money."

"What family?"

"It's a reference from a show in the 70's...Never mind. I'll just show you the reruns. What's up?"

He chortled. "Have you been drinking?"

"How can you tell?"

"You sound like it." The audible smile on his voice diminished as his tone descended to a serious note. "I just met with Davie and the PR Team. Let me first say to you that I'm not on board with the way they want to spin." He breathed into the phone heavily. "They want me to deny I'm married in interviews, and stage photos that elude I'm dating around."

I wasn't in the right frame of mind to pacify his frustration. I should have been mad when I heard his manager tell him to keep me a secret. Hearing it a second time made me hate the guy and I'd never met him.

"Maybe I should leave. Not because I want to, but because it's the right thing to do for your career. I mean let's face it. You wouldn't be in this mess if it weren't for me."

Mash seethed. "Rubbish."

"Everything would go back to normal if I wasn't in the picture."

"I said enough, Nadia. I'll handle this."

"How much have you had?"

I rambled. "Two. Two and a half. About to be three glasses."

"How dare you bring out Naughty Nadia when I'm not there. I wish you were here with me. I'd be all over you right now. Show me something to hold me over."

I flashed my breast then shrieked with embarrassment.

Mash grinned. "Perfection. I'll be on my way as soon as the final show is over. Go sleep off that buzz til Daddy comes home. Love you."

"Love you, too."

It pained me to be the root cause of his drama. The last thing I wanted was to be his downfall. When the alcohol wore off in the morning, I opened my notebook and wrote a pro and con list of our relationship.

I was halfway down the page when I received a notification on my phone. I had a new follower on social media, a few comments I hadn't responded to, and one missed call from Khai.

I sent her a message:

Call you later. Miss you much!

Next, I checked my social account. "Son of a bitch!"

Harv Legend followed me. The unread message was from

him. I clicked on it and skipped the words as my eyes focused on a photo of a woman and Mash in deep conversation.

My chest felt as though it could cave in. Like a house had fallen on me. I keeled over with a sharp pain throbbing from the back of my head to the front. The ache pierced like a yo-yo in every joint of my body. I screamed and threw my phone to the opposite side of the bed.

I jumped up and painted the floor with my slippers, dragging my feet while making up an explanation for what I saw to settle my nerves. I looked out of the window and caught a glimpse of myself in the glass. It was as if outside mimicked how I felt inside, as the rain depicted tears on my face before they fell. Like a broken record I chanted, *'This can't be happening. This can't be happening.'*

On the verge of collapse, the first tear fell. I dialed Mash. No answer. I called him a second time. No answer. I needed him to explain. To hear him say nothing happened last night, or the picture was taken before we met, or the photo was staged by his management without his consent. I needed something. Anything to make the pain go away. I needed to hear his voice tell me that he wasn't a lie I convinced myself was true.

I called him a third time. When he didn't answer, I examined the photograph with a fine tooth comb, cursing Harv Legend and his malice. I enlarged the picture, looking for the wedding band, the hotel name in the background, a date, a logo, or anything of significance that would tell me something about what I was seeing.

When I came up empty, I closed the picture and read what Harv wrote:

From what I saw tonight, you are fair game.
I told you Queens belong with Kings
@ me.

Immediately, my mind went back to what he said the morning he and Mash squared up in Copenhagen. *"Seems like you would have mentioned that last night. But then again..."*

I was wrecked wondering, *'What did he mean by that?'* The longer I didn't hear from Mash, the higher my blood pressure climbed. I felt trapped, duped, ridiculous, and enraged.

Harv had me put me in a corner. I would tell Mash about the photo and from whom it came. He'd lose his temper and the outcome would land him in more hot water, and I'd be at fault for telling him. If I didn't show him and he found out later somehow, I'd be deemed untrustworthy for hiding the message. Or worse, accused of conversing with the enemy behind his back. The blame would still fall on me.

I never felt more like a Black woman than in that moment—it was a tale as old as time, forever to blame no matter what. And feeling like the catalyst of Mash's downfall, I skipped being mad, jumped over angry, bypassed rage, and embraced crazy.

My mind created multiple scenarios with each passing minute Mash didn't return my call. I checked the time and wondered:

'Is he with her right now?
Is that why he's not answering my call?
Why the fuck would he play me like this?
Is this a staged photo his PR put together?
How can a person make you feel so loved,
and betray you at the same time?
This doesn't make sense.
What are my friends going to think?
God I look stupid. Again!
I know he loves me.
He treats me like any woman
would dream of being treated.
Will I ever know the truth?
I trusted him.
What the fuck is going on!
Why would he do this to me?'

Then it hit me. I'd seen the girl in the photo before. I ran to the bedroom and flipped through his albums, looking for the book with the models and famous people. There she was. Smiling in at least ten or more pictures with him.

I threw the album across the room and went into the kitchen. I cooked what hadn't been cooked, baked a casserole and a few of the cookies I'd rolled into balls earlier, whipped up a second flavor, ate some of the dough, baked a sourdough loaf, and sautéed peppers and onions to dress up a sandwich.

I stood against the island and took a bite, then burst into tears. I spit the perfectly dressed hoagie on the floor. I couldn't catch my breath. I wasn't this woman. I didn't want to be this woman. I didn't like this woman, as I had already been her years before.

The fairytale was over. What I thought Mash and I shared had been tainted. My okay life back home suddenly seemed better than the one I traded up for. I couldn't have been more wrong.

I packed what I could fit into two suitcases, and framed a picture of us in Italy that I'd stuck in the crevice of the mirror on the dresser. I placed it in the center of the pool table in the dining room, and said good-bye to the house I thought was going to be my home.

The taxi called for entry through the gate, and I lugged my bags outside and set the alarm. As the driver drove me away, a song I used to know so well came on the radio. I shook my head and sang along to it in my head. *'Good morning heartache, what's new.'*

better than the one [illegible] though I could do to this now.

I packed compulsively if only for something to do. I saw a
picture of us in Italy that I sold weeks ago. [illegible] circled the bottom
on the dresser I placed it in my pocket. [illegible] of the pool table in the
dining room, and said good-bye to the horse I thought was
going to be my horse.

The taxi pulled up early, though I thought, and I lugged my
bags, cushions, set the alarm. As the engine droned its syncopated
[illegible] I knew so well came [illegible] the [illegible] I knew I'd [illegible]
and [illegible] in my [illegible]. Good morning, he said [illegible] wide
awake.

REALISM

$\mathcal{T}$he credit from my cancelled flight came in handy. I caught the next flight into Denver, then waited two hours for a layover to GSP.

Once I landed in the States, I silenced my phone for a "peace" of mind and roamed the airport in search of the apocalyptic art people raved about. The white death horse topped the creepy as fuck displays.

Fires, coffins, and a weird looking children of the corn portrait were not on my bingo card. One mural was made of nightmares. It spooked me so bad that I went back to my gate, and was happy to get the hell out of Satan's airport.

CAROLINA. The real home of home. Mama's house. My voice of reason.

I don't think she's ever hugged me so tight, or so long. To be in her embrace soothed my bleeding soul, and just like that I felt like a little girl again.

Her house wasn't the house I grew up in, but the scent of it was the same. A blend of roasted coffee and baked goods lived inside the walls, with a hint of bleach and ammonia in the air.

We sat in the kitchen playing catch up, waiting for the timer to ding to take her sweet bread out of the oven. I turned my phone on to show her pictures of my travels with continuous interruptions of texts, calls, and voice messages.

"Something seems important. You ought to get that," she said.

"It can wait. I wanted to show you one picture in particular."

"Oh my. Weren't you a smashing bride." Ma held her chest. "When was this?"

"About a month ago."

"When do I get to meet my new son?"

I shrugged.

"Is this what you came home to tell me?"

I fidgeted. "Sort of?"

"Well, you don't need my approval because it's already done. And you know I was gonna tell you, you looked beautiful as ever. So, what is it?"

"I think it's over."

My mother laughed deep from her belly as the timer dinged. She removed the bread from the oven, and placed it on top of a towel on top of the toaster.

Sighing and making comical noises she asked, "Over. Already? Why?"

"It's a long story."

"It always is."

"And before you say it, I know marriage takes work but… We've hit a huge bump in the road."

"Is it that bad? Or are you making it that bad? Because honey to be honest, you look happy to me."

"I was happy, Ma. But I don't think I'm going back."

"What do you mean…Was? I know the look of love when I see it. Especially on my baby."

The phone rang again.

"Is that him?"

I nodded yes, unable to survive her stare.

"Talk to him."

"I need more time."

"Okay Ms. Need More Time. Some other woman is gonna take your time."

"One already has. I think."

Her eyes met up with mine. "Start from the beginning."

Lounging comfortably in my pajamas, I poured out my soul to my Mama. The highs and lows of the past few months. The hurt I felt about my dilemma.

She shared a story with me about perspective versus perception. "Sometimes things aren't what they seem, and without hearing what your husband has to say, you could be making a mistake. A picture is worth a thousand words."

I showed her the picture.

"People don't always have good intentions. Are you going to allow the person who sent you that photo to control your happiness?"

After making her point, she finished schooling me by saying as long as I knew the truth about the fake pictures, other people's insight shouldn't matter.

"People are gonna think whatever they wanna think anyway. And in a marriage, communication can make it, or break it." She handed me a slice of the warm bread.

I sat on the stool nearly healed from the taste of my mother's cooking, ready to hear my husband's explanation. I returned his call and he answered on the first ring, looking at me through the glass with seething eyes in utter silence.

"Hey," I mumbled.

He took a few seconds to respond. "What the fuck babe? I've been calling you all day."

I was shocked by his callous tone and word choice. "I turned off my ringer. I needed to figure some things out."

We sat in silence, waiting for the other to speak.

"Why did you leave?" he asked, in a softer tone than before. "Where are you and when are you coming home?"

"I'm at my mother's house, and I don't know the answer to that question."

"You have no idea how I'm feeling right now. I rushed home to be with you, and instead found you've left me. And for what?"

"For starters, I don't want you to resent me. I don't want to be the reason you lose everything you've worked for."

"I would never resent you. I told you to let me worry about work. Come home."

My heart rate increased and my palms began to sweat. There wasn't an easy way to ask him about the picture, so I blurted it out. "Did anything happen this weekend? Something I should hear from you and no one else?"

"I have no idea what you're talking about."

"Check your phone. I sent you something."

We stared at each other through our screens, waiting for the message to transmit. "Bloody hell. Where did you get this?"

"Harv sent it to me."

"Bollocks! That barmy maggot! Is this why you left?"

"Who is she?" I demanded.

"No one. Nadia, I don't know what else to do to show you I love you."

"I know you love me."

"Then why are you giving up on us so easily? I promise you. It's nothing. I will explain everything to you. But I want to do it in person. I need you to know I would never do anything to hurt you."

Having to wait for him to explain the image infuriated me. I didn't need an answer in person. I just needed clarity. My hesitation to answer his question bothered him, so he asked it again.

"You know I would never hurt you, right?"

I huffed and scowled at him. "That's what makes this so hard. I believe you. It's a lot to take in, but I honestly believe you. What confuses me is the picture, and the things Harv says. In Copenhagen, he made that remark about you, and now he's saying from what he saw I'm now fair game? All of this code language makes me wonder what he's not saying."

"He's being a dick. I'll take care of him. You, take some time. You did say you were homesick, so do whatever it is you need to do, then come back to me. I'll tell you everything. Do you still love me?"

"I wouldn't be hurt if I didn't love you."

The pain in my chest didn't leave after we spoke. It felt like a wrecking ball knocked the wind out of me, and left a huge dent in between my breasts. I was more confused than when I left, and tossed all night with a cloudy mind.

I beat the sun and my mother up the next morning, and suggested we drive to Goose Creek to pay my Grams a visit.

"She'll love that surprise."

Ma skimmed through my phone, admiring the photos of my travels while I sped down 26. I arrived at the retirement village in record time.

Ma shook her head. "You've got a lead foot just like your grandmother."

After two and a half hours of listening to the oldies at the crack of dawn, we signed our names in the record book, and I power-walked to my grandmother's room. Seeing her never failed to brighten my day, and I was long overdue for one of her hugs.

I peeped my head into her room. She sat in her rocking chair, dressed comfortably in a blush sweat suit with her long, silver silky hair pulled behind her ears in two braids. I was jealous my hair never grew as long as hers, but I did inherit her texture and wave pattern, which made up for what I lacked.

"There is my pretty lady?" I said, entering her room.

She turned to her side and looked at me, fanning her hand and turning up her top lip.

"Well, gal why didn't you tell me you were coming? It's been a long time." She kissed my cheeks. "You still got a little sugar in there."

"You know I love surprising you," I said, kissing her forehead.

I held onto her tightly, smelling her perfume from the 1950's mixed with mink oil, and dove soap.

She patted me on the shoulder. "Yes, you sure do. You look good, gal. Skin so plump and smooth."

"I am the chocolate version of you."

"Which is even better. Less wrinkles when you get old."

Ma finally arrived in the room. "Leave some hugs for me."

Grams turned towards her and gave mom her cheek. "Oh, I got both of you today. Is the good-looking boy with you, too?"

"Momma behave."

"You know I will do no such thing."

I told her I came alone and she asked to see another picture of Mash. I pulled up some of our travel photos, and showed her how to swipe left and right.

"This sure is from the future." She scoffed, then arrived at the one of us in Barcelona. "Nadia, you are every bit of me I tell you what. I would've married him too if it was safe back in my day. My baby girl snagged her a husband. Such a handsome boy. Grams can dig it."

"Momma." My mother droned.

"What *chile*? You are always cramping my style." Grams pointed at her. "You know that's why I won't come live with her. I'd never get to see my boyfriends if I moved in her jailhouse."

"Did you say boyfriends with an s?" I asked.

"You heard me right. I have one on every hall in here."

"How is that possible?" my Mama asked.

"Easy. One is a nighthawk, one is in a wheelchair, and the other one can't half see."

I curled over in laughter. "I've missed you so so much, Grams?"

"If they have men my age over there who look like your man, I'll move in with you, baby girl. Book my ticket tonight."

"Momma please. You aren't moving anywhere."

Grams kissed her teeth. "You hear the sheriff talkin'?"

"Okay. I'm ringing the bell. You two always go at it. How have you been doing?"

"Really good today, but I have my days, arthritis and all."

"You feel like getting out of here today?" I asked.

"Hell yeah, if you're not too tired. I wanna see the water. I can smell it for God's sake, so I'd like to see it."

I grabbed her sweater. "Let's go."

On our way to the beach, I noticed The Creek had been updated since my last visit. I remembered it as nine busy streets surrounded by green landscape and moss trees. Now mom and pop businesses and shopping plazas stood in lots that were once flat grassed terrain. The amount of street lights doubled if not tripled, and the population and diversity was significantly on the rise.

In less than an hour, Grams removed her shoes and walked barefoot in the sand until she reached the water. She looked like a young woman as she played footsie with the waves and dusting off seashells. I could tell from her smile she was reminiscing about old times, and mom and I watched her become one with the sand as the grains sifted between her toes.

I joined her in the water, while Mom stood in line at the booth for chair rentals. Grams and I were in sync, and she hurried in one of our special talks while we had a few moments alone.

"My gal went and got married on me," she said.

"Are you mad finding out this way?"

"Not at all. All I care about is you being happy. Are you happy?"

"That's a complicated answer, Grams. I love him though."

"Hell, I would love him, too. But happiness is what I want for you."

"I'm happy, we just have a few wrinkles that need ironing."

"I'm sure you'll tell me all about it when you're ready. Just remember. You ain't nobody's fool. If you can't get the wrinkles out, get a new shirt. Uh oh, here comes the warden."

Listening to the waves roar a few feet away, we stretched beneath three rented beach chairs and umbrellas. Basking in the breeze with worthy conversation between three generations for hours, I forgot about my dilemma for a short while. My mind needed that break, and my soul needed what my grandmother had always given me—strength.

Once the sun set, we grabbed a quick bite to eat, and said good-bye to Grams. We headed back upstate where I spent a few more days with my mother, then I returned to Charlotte, to the abandoned place I called my own.

Khai had done a great job taking care of my plants. I did a thorough walkthrough, dusting what needed to be dusted, changed the linens to fresh washed sheets, tossed the spoiled milk from the fridge, sorted my mail, and settled in.

I pulled out my laptop and stared at a blank page, not knowing where to begin, and realizing I had nothing to come back to except loneliness.

Before the five o'clock traffic jam, I surprised Khai at work.

They said the weed man is in here." I teased, when I popped my head in her office.

"Oh my God! What are you doing here?! Is this why you didn't call me back?!"

We hugged.

My eyes grew big when I remembered that I forgot to return

her missed call the day the chaos erupted. "It slipped my mind. My bad. Ain't you happy to see me?"

"Of course. But what's with the surprise? I could have picked you up from the airport."

"This trip was a spur of the moment thing."

"Is Mash with you?"

"No, he had to work."

"So, we can get some girl time in?"

"Yes. I'm in desperate need."

We met the girls at one of the better, upscale clubs in the city for happy hour. While we waited for them to arrive, Khai ordered appetizers and the first round of drinks, filling me in on what her phone call was about.

"Taylor and Levi are having marital problems, but no one knows why. And, my father-in-law moved in with me and B, so I've been using your house as an escape."

"As if I would complain about that."

Before she finished telling me about the strain the new tenant has put on her marriage, Shannon walked through the door.

"What's up, Grandma Klump? You remembered us little people."

I stood to hug her, then Isla popped up and waved her hand. "Lady Nadia has decided to grace us with her presence. To what do we owe the pleasure?" She said in a fake British accent.

I rolled my eyes. "It's good to see you too, Isla."

We air kissed cheek to cheek as Taylor surprised me from behind.

"You finally came home." She squeezed my shoulders.

"It took me a minute, but I finally made it. Now give me all the tea."

Shannon lit up like a light bulb, describing her latest boy toy while Isla kept the details of her mystery man a secret.

"How are you and Levi doing?" I asked Taylor.

She moaned something jumbly under her breath and deflected. "How is London?"

"I don't know. It was great at first, but now...I have a lot of decisions to make."

"Would these decisions have to do with you getting married and not telling us." Taylor snitched.

"How did you know?"

"We all know. Mash told Levi, and Levi swore me to secrecy, but you know I had to tell the girls."

"I wanted to tell y'all in person, and show you the ring his mother passed down to me. Y'all wanna see pictures?"

They passed my phone around and swiped while I gave them the details of Barcelona. How Mash proposed. How beautiful our honeymoon in Italy was. And how I made my head wrap for our ceremony.

Taylor's face turned glum. "Look at you with those flowers in your hair. Levi and I should have done this. Simple, intimate and romantic."

I said, "Your wedding was beautiful, Tay."

Everyone at the table synchronized to pacify her.

She scoffed. "I guess."

Khai gave me the side eye. I pretended she hadn't warned me of their trouble in paradise, but it was clear something was going on with them.

Taking the negative light off of Taylor, I mentioned Mash's management wants us to keep the marriage a secret—curious to see how they would respond, and who would agree with me.

Taylor said, "I say go along with the lie. His image is his livelihood, and from what I saw, it's worth it to lie."

"Sorry." Isla chimed in. "I would want everyone to know I'm the wife."

Khai asked, "What does Mash have to say about all of this?"

"He says I'm not a secret and not to worry. But I feel like I'm in his way."

"Did he say that?" She continued.

"No."

Shannon tapped my hand. "Then stop doing the Nadia thing and jumping to conclusions."

I pouted. "The Nadia thing?"

"You know what you do," they said in unison.

I clutched my fake pearls at their synchronized depiction of me. "So, I'm thousands of miles away, and still the butt of the joke?"

Both of my brows raised. They waited for me to laugh, but I made them sweat for a bit.

"Naive Nadia is now No Shit Nadia." I paused before I cackled.

They joined in and we carried on as if nothing had changed over the months I was away. But something had.

Me.

At that moment, I decided not to tell them about the picture. The old me would have blabbed every detail, and sought their advice. The new me had grown up a little since the last time they saw me, and she recognized it was best to keep some things to herself.

"Oh, okay," he said. She muttered.

"Shut up," she hissed. "Hey," ... stepping over the walk ... from
...and things to remember.
...upon it?" ... I've had time.

"You know what you do," I said ... in a minute.

...behind my spare parts at ... pickup of ... pickup of
...not be comfortable is of ... new, and still the hurt of the
later.

Both of my brows raised, I knew we'd ... for me to laugh out ...
...mattress within that bed.

"Now that's a kiss now," he said. "Yeah," I said. I raised before I
asked.

...I grinned in and we waited in that tent of ... had obtained ...
...over the while I answered. But something had ...

A strange thought I decided not to tell them about ... the future.
...I held me that I would have hidden ... don't know ... and sought that
place. The men are now shown up a little up of the last time
...the crew ... said the receptionist was just to keep some things
to be, said.

ARRIVEDERCI

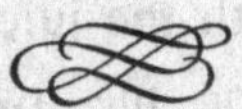

'd done what I intended. I cured the homesick feeling, checked in on my folks, and caught up with my friends. My checklist was almost complete with one new addition to cross out. I still had to hear Mash out and then decide if what he said was more believable than what I saw with my own eyes.

The morning came with a hangover from hell and the burning question regarding what I should do. Lying back on my favorite Egyptian count sheets, I had one eye open, and the other closed like Uncle Fester.

The doorbell rang and woke me up. Slowly, I robed and opened the door, greeted by orchids at my feet. I shouted to the delivery man at the end of the sidewalk.

"Wait! I'll get you a tip!"

He waved me off. "No need! It's already been taken care of! Thanks!"

I picked up the arrangement and read the card:

'Counting the days ~ Love Mash'

The color of my morning surprise looked good on the end table in the living room. I left them there, then grabbed a juice and toasted a stale bagel from the fridge. I took a bite and threw it in the garbage. Hanging on the wall above the trash can was my calendar. The date was circled in red, which meant there was a group meeting later on at 7 o'clock.

I rinsed my mouth with the juice, staring at the date. My stomach growled, breaking me away from my thoughts. I searched for something else to snack on and took the crackers I found upstairs. I climbed back into bed and texted Mash:

> I love you, too.

I ate a few crackers then reacquainted myself with my sheets. It was hours later when I woke from hunger pains. I threw on a fitted sweatsuit to drive across town to my favorite mom and pop pizza parlor. My taste buds deserved a pinch of heaven.

Bell and banana peppers, onions, and cheese on a soft doughy crust tasted just as I remembered. I closed my eyes as the flavor soothed my soul. I was reminded of Italy. I compared it to the best pizza I ever had in life. And though Mash wasn't there with me physically, I still felt him near me and accepted his presence would never leave me.

With a full stomach and a to-go box of leftovers, I drove a few streets over to the Dr. Bartley sessions. I sat in the parking lot, noting some new faces mixed in with the old ones I talked about mercilessly months ago. My hand was on the handle of the door when Taylor asked if I was free. I took it as a sign that I was somewhere I didn't need to be.

I arrived at Taylor's twenty minutes later. The tension between her and Levi was so thick that a knife wouldn't suffice to cut it. She spoke in circles—never truly offering what drove the wedge between her and Levi. Seeing how miserable she was reminded me of a saying Grams said all the time, *'If God took all the problems and threw them in the air, everyone would grab their own.'*

Their quarrel prompted me to call London. I was ready to hear his explanation and make my decision to avoid being the company misery loved to keep. I was met with deja vu. He didn't answer my call.

The next morning, I shopped for groceries and prepared my homemade salsa and guac for bowling night. A night surrounded by my friends was better than sitting alone in the house wondering why I hadn't heard from my husband.

The crowd at the alley was mixed with new and old faces. Some I recognized from the wedding. The others I couldn't place. The best man from the wedding caught my attention by making a joke at my expense.

"Hey, Mrs. Copperfield. One minute I saw you in London, then the next minute you vanished."

"Sounds like me. Drew, right? Levi's college buddy?"

"Yeah. I asked about you a few times, but Levi said I moved too slow. He said you stayed over there and got married?"

"I did."

"Was it the guy you were dancing with?"

"You saw us?"

"Everyone did."

I smiled, remembering Khai said the exact same thing to me.

Brian, Khai's husband, tapped his shoulder. "Time to whoop ass! No fraternizing with the competition."

Drew winked at him. "Well, congratulations, and good luck tonight."

"Your team's the one who needs it."

We separated into teams and began the competition—Mars versus Venus. Alcohol induced laughs, and gin induced verbal brawls made for a good night. At the end of the first round, the women led on the scoreboard. The losers stormed the bar to buy the next round of drinks.

Shannon talked below the music, but loud enough to be heard. "They say when you get married you become more desirable. Is that true, Nadia?"

"I'm gonna say, yes."

"Me, too," Khai added. "I've had men come at me *outta* the woodworks, but the gag is those men wouldn't marry a soul. They just want to fuck you and send you back home."

Everyone gasped.

I tapped her leg. "Khai! You cursed!"

She fanned us off. "Well, it's true."

Shannon added. "Women are no different. They want to sleep with your man just so they can stare you down and throw it in your face."

Isla placed her straw in her mouth. "You would know."

Shannon gave Isla the look of death, then danced in her face.

Taylor interrupted the two of them going at it. "Why are we talking about this?"

We looked to one another, realizing we were close to getting answers of what was going on in her house. Shannon opened her mouth to explain when Khai changed the subject.

"I heard Isla went hummus shopping."

Isla hid her face, then looked at me. "I don't know how you do it. We had nothing in common."

"You have to get the right one," I said.

"By the way, our friends want us to fix whatever's going on between us. Are we good?" Isla asked.

"We're good." I held out my hand to shake for a truce.

"Ladies, get your pretty asses up! We're about to redeem ourselves!" Levi announced.

Team Venus went toe to toe with Team Mars throwing strikes, turkeys, talking trash, and celebrating with in-your-face choreographed routines. The men drank so much beer, we thought we had an edge on them until the final frame, where we lost by a gutter ball from our weakest link.

The party continued at Khai's house. Brian cranked up the grill. Khai brought games outside by the pool. And Shannon's new beau took charge of the music.

As I watched the couples interact, happily and miserably, I realized I was ready to go home. Not to the one a few blocks over. The one on the cusp of daylight, with the man I wanted to be happy and miserable with.

Stepping away from the party, I eased over by the fence for privacy. I finally made contact with Mash, but he sounded off. His answers were short and vague, and he sounded on edge speaking with me. It felt like I was talking to a stranger, especially when I didn't get an I love you at the end. I told the girls I was calling it a night.

"Don't go," said Khai. "Why would you leave us being together to go mope around in your house?"

She knew me well because that's exactly what I was going to do. To throw her off my scent, I convinced myself to stay for another hour when I was losing it on the inside. But as powerful as the mind is, the heart is stronger, and the two of them collaborating is unbeatable.

The sting of tears formed in my eyes. I held them back for as long as I could. I couldn't hang around for another hour. I had to get out of there and hop on the next plane to London. I needed answers of why Mash suddenly turned cold on me when I was the wounded one.

Shannon's friend then put on a Bob Marley song. It wasn't Chances Are, but it still made me think of Mash.

Water rushed to my eyelids, and I didn't want anyone to see me cry. I did the unthinkable and kicked off my shoes, took a deep breath and jumped in the pool. Below the water I heard the commotion of screams.

"Somebody go in there and get her!"

"She doesn't know how to swim!"

Three seconds under, I rose to the top. "Yes, I do!"

I swam from one side to the other as my friends grew louder and louder. I reached up for the edge and pulled myself to the surface. My eyes tightened from the chlorine dripping from my hair. I stood in the shallow to clear my face.

"So, you're a show off now," his deep voice rang in my ear.

I opened my eyes to Mash kneeling before me. The huge smile on his face made me grin from ear to ear.

"Hey you," I said, lifting myself higher to meet his lips as fast as I could. "What are you doing here?"

He pulled me out of the water. "I came to bring you home."

My soaked clothing dampened his as I pressed against him, locking my lips with his as if it were for the first time. Chatter in the background didn't break my concentration. I was in the arms of the one I wanted to be with, and didn't let go of his tongue until our hosts put an end to our moment.

"Get a room!" They shouted. "Alright. Alright. That's enough of that!"

I turned to my girls. "Who knew he was coming here?"

"Just me," said Levi. "My wife can't keep a secret."

I gave him a fist motion with a smile on my face.

"Levi, you said it was hot down here. You should have said boiling." Mash joked.

He removed his shirt and his shoes, then picked me up. I wrapped my legs around him, hugged him tight around his neck, and screamed as he leaped into the pool.

My eyes closed when I felt the water on my feet, but I opened them once Mash pinched me, and kissed him underwater. We rose from the deep end, my arms still around him, spinning and playing in the water.

"Get in y'all!" I convinced the others to join us.

The night ended with a splash party. Soaking wet, we took

the party back to my house, skipped the tour, and went straight to my bedroom—Our bedroom.

I was in a rush to feel him inside of me, but he took his time to give me what I wanted.

"Shower's in there?" He pointed.

I opened the door for him.

He turned it on, then undressed me while the water heated up. In the shower, he shampooed my hair, building up a sensual, sexual tension that was hard to resist. The slip of suds barely seeped between us with him pressed so close to my back.

I was in agony, yearning for our bodies to collapse into each other. He kissed me after every rinse, teasing me with finger play in between. I shuddered from the cold air blowing above, then warmed with heat when he tasted my quivering lips between my thighs.

I turned my back to him, but he had something else in mind. He lifted me between my legs and carried me to the bed. On my knees, I fell atop my good satin spread, and he held me in place grazing my ass cheeks with his teeth.

He spread them apart and wet his fingers, massaging my forbidden with gentle, circular strokes. Screams of passion parted my lips as my face was buried to muffle my cry. I wailed in ecstasy until he laid me on my back.

I squirmed even though I hungered for him.

"You remember how to take it. Look at me," he said, and submitted his plow.

I clutched on to him as tight as I could, moaning and sighing in his ear.

"Good girl." He grunted, then dug deeper and faster. "Oh, how I've missed your sugar."

He abruptly shifted me on my side and pulled me to the edge of the bed. Towering over me like a lighthouse, he dug inside my waters sideways, and yowled at the touch of a newfound corner. I spread my ass cheeks open so he could see his excavation. That move heightened his intensity. He galloped strong charges that made my womb throb and held onto my shoulders to place his release where he pleased.

My drip held his load as he recovered, clutching and vibrating on his wood. Making him weaker and weaker until he could no longer stand. "Wherever we are together is home," he said, falling beside me. And that's where I belonged—At his side because he was home for me.

His hands ran through my hair, then all over my body. "How do you feel?"

"Like all's right with the world."

"It is now." He kissed the back of my hand. "I missed you. I baked the cookies you left in the fridge, and laughed to myself at how you only eat the crispy ends and give me the middle, yet with cake you only eat the middle and give me the end trimmings." He chortled. "I can't make sense of it."

"I know I'm quirky."

"Yes, you are. But I fell in love with quirky."

"I'm already lying here naked. You don't have to flatter me."

He rolled me on top of him, sweeping my face and reading my eyes. I played with the stubble on his chest, holding my words and putting him to sleep. I laid my head on his shoulder and gave in to the night. We were both tired. But I was still owed a conversation.

In the morning, he stroked my hair to wake me.

"I signed with new management."

"Is that a good move for you?"

"For us. And yes. Now, we can move on from the nonsense that's come between us."

"Mash, I don't want to be kept a secret. I thought I could handle it, but..."

"You don't have to. We're out in the open. No more secrets."

"And Cardiff?"

"Nadia."

"Just tell me nothing happened so I can stop thinking about it."

"Nothing happened. Harv and I used to be close mates. He knows I despise her. He saw it as a way to get back at me. He's reaching at its finest."

"That picture filled my head with all sorts of wild theories. And when you didn't answer your phone, I believed it. It hurt to feel conflicted like that. Especially when you know deep down the person you love wouldn't hurt you, but then get blindsided with an image of that person with someone else. I looked at that picture over and over and started to doubt myself. Doubt us."

He sat up. "What Harv sent you was me telling her that I would file a restraining order if she came to any more of my shows."

"Who is she?"

"An old friend."

"And she was in Copenhagen, am I right?"

"Yes. But can we not talk about her? She is nothing. You are everything."

"Okay. If I'm everything. I was thinking, since we're both here we might as well file for a marriage license, so I can change my last name before we go back."

He raised up and pulled my face to his. "I love that idea, Mrs. Sharper."

♡✈

THE COURTHOUSE WASN'T good enough for Ma. She met her son-in-law and welcomed him to the family. When we returned from filing the papers, she made one request. The Sunday before we left the States, we wed in her church with Ma, Grams, and the girls as our witness.

Mash surprised me with written vows. He found the pro and

187

con list I wrote about our relationship the night I was in distress.

To the congregation he said, "I won't read everything on this paper, because I've crossed out the things that don't matter. My wife needed several reassurances of my love for her, and being the analytical person she is, she compiled a list. I found that list, and carry it with me everyday for good luck. I want my wife to know that her list is also my list, and it reads:

> She makes me happy. I have grown as a person because of her, and having her in my life has changed me for the better. And I love her. I love her. I love her. She also wrote that I taught her how to swim, but I would like to add, she taught me what it is to be happy. With her love, I am complete.

Ma's pastor didn't get a chance to say, '*You may now kiss your bride*'. Mash reeled me in like a winding rod and kissed me before the words left his mouth, and we became husband and wife again. But this time, I had no reservations about living abroad. I was ready to leave my old life behind with an incomparable man that was worthy of me, and write a new chapter in a new place I now call home.

THE LIST

Cons: ~~Interference with career, drama with colleagues, jealousy, financially challenged.~~

Pros: *Makes me happy, changed for the better, grown as a person, sleep better next to him, taught me to swim, I love him, I love him, I love him.*

Thank you for diving into my fictional worlds. These characters reappear in a mashup novella with the cast featured from my On Track But Off Course Series, 'My Gift To You: Levi & Launa Find Love'. https://books2read.com/mygifttoyou

facebook.com/t.k.richards

instagram.com/t.k.richards

tiktok.com/@tkrwrites

youtube.com/tkrichards

pinterest.com/tkwrites

SNEAK PEEK OF BOOK 2 - A TASTE OF THE FORBIDDEN

Chapter One
Brand New Me

I hadn't missed the clouds of cigarette smoke in the clubs, but I did miss seeing Mash come alive onstage, and my guilty pleasure of people watching. After a few peach flavored drinks, I got a little loose and danced provocatively against the railing near the stage. Mash blushed at me grooving solo in my corner, so I simmered down, and fought the urge to move to the beat.

The ambiance of the crowd, the loud sounds of the bass booming from the speaker, and Mash focusing on his work suddenly turned me on.

Oh how I love a working man. Who doesn't?

I fanned myself with a club flyer to cool down and shy away my raised nipples piercing through my top. The peach schnapps and vodka also played a role in my sudden yearning to be pillaged by my husband hard at work.

I turned away from the crowd until my boobs were no longer on high beam, then refaced the stage to continue watching the show.

Mash winked at me. My face flushed from his flirtation.

Oh shit. He knows that I'm heavily aroused.

To keep my nipples from telling the world I am in need for some action and the naughty thoughts flashing in my head at bay, I crowd surfed the faces from the atrium section. The horde was heavily engaged with the music. Shades of partygoers below the color changing LED lights were enjoying themselves. Some more than others. But the vibe I felt from one of the faces in the crowd didn't come across as friendly.

A woman stared me down for far too long. If she could shoot venom at me from that distance, I'd be poisoned.

Her gaze was beyond intense when we locked eyes. So extreme that a chill traveled down my spine, and my skin felt like it froze amidst the heat in the club.

I waited for her to blink, but her menacing face didn't budge because she wanted my attention. And I didn't break my gaze either, letting her know that I didn't scare easily.

She finally folded, and I turned toward the stage, cheering on my husband who decided to play my favorite song. Suddenly, it dawned on me. I recognized the woman. Her silhouette, long face, and dark eyes screamed at me from the back of my mind. She was the mysterious woman in the photograph Mash and I never discussed. The bitch I wondered about from time to time. Mostly when I was pouting over something silly.

How do I play this? I thought. *Should I lock eyes with her again? Then, roll them when she stares back? Or do something clever to make her jealous?*

Jealousy won.

Winding my hips on the side of the stage, I eye-fucked *my husband*. His face turned pink and red, and his interaction with the crowd took a pause as he bit the side of his lip. His smoldering features turned serious as he signaled to some guy behind him, pressed a button on his equipment, then stepped forward in my direction.

His hands wrapped around my waist to still me from winding my hips. "I see Naughty Nadia came here tonight. You wanna quick one backstage?"

I moaned in his ear and smirked at the girl in the crowd studying us from below. She squinted her eyes as I showcased my effect on the man she obviously came to see. But he was with me.

If she didn't know me before, she knew me now, but I still knew nothing about her. Something told me I was about to learn more than I wanted to, but that lesson would have to wait, as I was beguiled with the man who put a ring on my finger. Naughty Nadia was at the party, and she wanted pleasure, even if it was against the dirty wall of a dressing room.

I placed my bag around the knob before Mash locked the door behind us. Forcefully, I unbuttoned his pants, and yanked down his zipper. He was ready without any participation on my part.

I stroked his penis in my hands as his face pressed against mine, then we fervidly locked in a sloppy kiss. I could feel the speed of his heart increase with my hands wrapped around his gyrating muscle beating like a marching band.

His fingers slipped between my orifice. "I knew you wanted me twenty minutes ago," he said, gliding my drip around the apex of my inner thighs.

Quickly, I dropped low and wet his wanton whistle. He sighed of gratification as I licked him with a circular motion of my tongue, then enclosed his head in my mouth for one quick suck.

"Ha-ah-ih," he respired, running his fingers through my hair.

I rose to face him. "See, there you go. Getting excited trying to mess up my hair. You'll get more of that later tonight."

He pressed my back against the door and lifted my right leg. I exhaled in heat, anxious to feel his girth separate my walls.

A gentle tug on my thong bared my pulsing flesh for his dick to stand up in my pussy with ease. Above my head, he gurgled sounds of pleasure from the tightness of my warm embrace hugging his sturdy stride breaking me open.

He grunted, and I whined, bracing myself for the lashing my pussy was happy to receive.

I clenched my juices to coat him and moaned. He groaned as his strong, long thrusts withdrew screams from my mouth like the people on the opposite side of the door enjoying the show.

"You know how to make me come quick. Don't you girl?" He sighed, then tongued me as he approached his peak.

I timed each push and pull until I was lost in the zone of our souls being weaved together. Then, he came inside of me, breathing heavily against my cheek, holding me tighter than a bear hugging a tree.

Unable to move I asked, "You good?"

"When I'm with you, always." He slid out of me gently. "You?"

"You won't hear me complain." I searched for a napkin in my bag. "You better get back out there." I jittered from a cramp forming in my toe, then lined the tissue around the seat of my thong. "I'll be out shortly."

Mash frowned, securing the zipper on his jeans. "I wouldn't dare leave you back here alone."

I rushed to make myself presentable, then we headed back to the stage arm in arm. The audience cheered at his return under the flashing lights, and he reveled in it, holding up his hands with a proud grin on his lips.

I cheered for him, too, but mostly for the private performance I had just received.

For the remainder of his set I behaved. No provocative dancing. No enticing him from the side of the stage. I sat patiently in the seat I was provided, and played the role of a good supportive wife while scouring the crowd for the hateful eyes piercing through me moments ago.

They say seek and you shall find. And that is exactly what I did with the ghost of my husband's past. A rising problem I sensed that returned to haunt me.

REVIEWS ENCOURAGE VORACIOUS INTEREST EVERY WHERE TO SUPPORT

ME, THE AUTHOR

I GREATLY APPRECIATE IT

XOXO

T.K. RICHARDS

STEAMY ROMANCE & WOMEN'S FICTION

T.K. Richards is a multi-genred author telling stories of strong heroines who navigate love without losing themselves in the pursuit. She writes contemporary romance, love stories & women's fiction filled with plot twists, witty banter, and heavy spice.

Choose Your Favorite

Pick Your Preference

FRIENDS TO LOVERS   ENEMIES TO LOVERS   ROMANCE   LOVE STORY

Which MMC Is Your Fave

PARANORMAL HERO   STREET SAVVY   BUSINESS SAVVY   ROCK STAR   SPORTS STAR

Pick A Trope

LOVE TRIANGLE   SLOWBURN ROMANCE   INSTALOVE   COLLEGE GIRL FMC

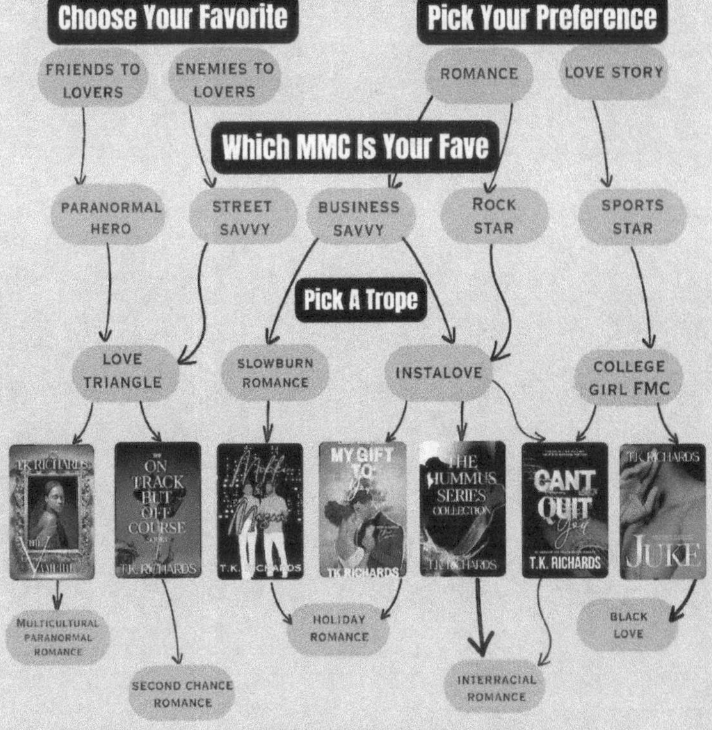

MULTICULTURAL PARANORMAL ROMANCE   HOLIDAY ROMANCE   BLACK LOVE

SECOND CHANCE ROMANCE   INTERRACIAL ROMANCE

WWW.TKRICHARDS.COM

T.K. RICHARDS is a multi-genre author with popular novels and novellas in several genres of romance including Black, Interracial/Multicultural & Paranormal Romance, Speculative Fiction, Women's Fiction, and Domestic Thrillers.

A graduate of Limestone University, T.K. has honors in Expository Writing, and was also the Poet Laureate of her graduating class. When she is not writing, she is immersed in the world of tennis, and binge watching movies—mostly comedy as she loves to laugh.

For more information about **T.K. Richards**, visit her website at www.tkrichards.com and subscribe to her newsletter at: https://tkrichardsnewsletter.ck.page

Follow **T.K. RICHARDS** on the platforms listed below to interact with her personally:

instagram.com/t.k.richards
Tkrichards.substack.com
pinterest.com/TKWrites
tiktok.com/@tkrwrites
youtube.com/tkrichards
goodreads.com/T.k.richards
bookbub.com/authors/t-k-richards
amazon.com/author/Tkrichards
patreon.com/tkrichards
bsky.app/profile/tkrichards

9 781959 253204